RED ARROWS

LAURA BURTON
JESSIE CAL

BURTON & BURCHELL LTD

COPYRIGHT

This book is written in U.S. English

Edited by: Susie Poole

Cover Design: Writing Avalanche

❀ Created with Vellum

CHAPTER 1

*R*ed sucked in a breath and tugged on her dress. She hated corsets and would have been much happier wearing her leather boots and pants with a loose shirt. But it was Aria's coronation day, and the whole kingdom had turned up in their finest clothes.

She walked along the grounds, smiling at all boughs of red and white flowers. The castle had been restored from all of the destruction by The Evil Queen, and it was as if she had never resided there. Red cast her eyes about, taking in the sight of the lush green trees and the gardens filled with blooms of every color.

It was like she had stepped into the most beautiful art canvas. An excitable chatter caught her attention as she approached the back of a crowd, and Red's heart fluttered. There was a buzz in the air and it was contagious. Red shouldered her way through the people and made for the main hall.

A guard stopped her. "Name?"

"Ryding Hood," she muttered, not bothering to add that she was mostly known as *Red*, thanks to the dumb nickname that Will Scarlet had given her. The guard stepped aside, and she walked in, looking up at the high ceiling in awe. Ice fractals hung like chandeliers, and the stone floor was covered in snow. Jack stood tall at the front of the hall, beside the high priest.

If Red hadn't known any better, she would have thought she had stepped into a wedding. Rows of wooden benches sat on either side of the hall, leaving an aisle in the middle. Red took a seat near the front and listened to the string quartet playing a classic song.

Excited whispers flew around the hall, and Red watched Jack, who stared ahead, unmoving. He looked different. His once dark hair was white as snow, and there was something about his countenance that seemed off to Red. What had happened to him? He didn't look human anymore. Many rumors spread through the kingdom about Aria. One of them was that she had turned Jack into a snowman. She laughed to herself at that one.

But he *had* changed. Despite his serious stance, his eyes brightened, and he broke into a broad grin. The song ended and a happier one picked up. Everyone rose to their feet and Red followed suit. Sighs and gasps filled the air. Red stood on her tiptoes to see over the heads, but she could only make out blonde hair.

Then she leaned to the side just as Aria passed her. Red gasped along with the other guests. She was beautiful.

Aria stood at the front and kneeled as Jack stepped aside. The high priest handed her a silver orb, then placed a golden crown on her head. When she rose, she turned around and looked out. To Red's surprise, her face was solemn and serious. There was not a hint of a smile on her red lips.

"All hail Queen Aria. May her days be long and her reign peaceful."

The guests repeated the priest's words then broke out into applause. Music played and a frosting of snow fell from the ceiling. Red held out her hand and caught the snowflakes, staring in wonderment.

Moments later, at the castle courtyard, huge banquet tables were laid out with all manner of food and drink. The guests filed into the courtyard and broke into excited chatter. Red took the opportunity to make her way out and catch up to Aria, who was leaving with Jack.

"Aria, wait."

Red joined Aria on the staircase. She turned and smiled, but it didn't reach her eyes. "Ry." They embraced for a moment, then she squeezed her arm as they broke apart. "What are you doing here? I thought you'd be with Robin."

"They're ready for you, my queen," one of the guards announced from the top of the staircase, and Aria turned away without so much as a goodbye. Something was wrong.

Red followed her up the staircase and to the balcony. Snow, who was Aria's sister, stood next to George, holding his hand, while Jack waited for Aria to join him.

Red made her way to Snow as Aria stepped forward, and the sound of cheers and whistles exploded into the air. *Aria is a natural at this*, Red thought as she watched her waving her hand so delicately. She rested a hand on the edge of the balcony and stood poised while Jack looked on.

"My dear people of the Chanted Kingdom." Aria's voice boomed with authority. "You have suffered greatly under the reign of The Evil Queen. But now, it is time for you to finally get what you deserve."

More cheers. Aria edged next to George and put a hand on his shoulder. She leaned in and whispered something, and he responded with a puzzled look. Red wondered if it was an apology for calling his mother evil.

But then, without warning, Aria grasped his back and knocked him over the edge of the balcony. Snow gasped, grabbing Red's arm. The crowd fell into a horrified silence as the sound of George's screams was halted by a splash. Red leaned over the edge and watched in horror as the lake swallowed him up.

Jack glanced at Aria in shock, but the new queen appeared unfazed. She threw out her hands, and an icy blast hit the lake, freezing it whole. Snow fell to her knees and screamed like a banshee. Aria turned away, unable to look. But then she sucked in a breath and straightened her posture.

"People of the Chanted Kingdom," Aria called out again. "The days of The Evil Queen may be over. But now, it is time for the rule of The Snow Queen."

Red stared at Aria's cold demeanor, stunned. She no longer recognized her friend. Instead, a cold-blooded monster stood before her.

Jack carefully picked up a crying Snow off the floor and rushed her inside. People screamed as they frantically ran away from Aria's blasts of ice. But then she began to pile mountains of snow all around the lake, and Red watched in horror as she blasted each of them to life. They opened their empty eyes and roared like an army of ice ogres.

The ground trembled under Red's feet, and she grabbed onto the balcony's ledge so as not to lose her balance.

"Aria!" Red called out over the chaos, and whatever was left of her friend met her eyes. "Please, don't do this."

Aria's face softened for a moment, and Red held hope at the sight of her misty eyes. But then Aria's face hardened again. "Run," she said in a deadly whisper.

Without another word, Red jumped off the ledge, then used the vines that hugged the walls to climb down. The thick cotton skirt of her dress snagged on a thorn. She wrenched at it, tearing the magenta material, and an icy breeze swept up her legs. She cursed under her breath and vowed to never wear a dress again. Once her feet hit the ground, she darted into the panicked crowd, running west into the woods.

Another ground-shaking roar came from behind her, and the ferocious blast of icy wind that accompanied it thrust her to the earthy floor. She whipped her head around and looked up at one of the ice ogres marching toward her. The ground trembled beneath her hands with each step.

She staggered to her feet, picked up her skirts, then stumbled toward a nearby bush. Shoving her hand behind the overgrown plant, she searched for her bow and arrow, not daring to look back. Her fingers grazed the strap, and she pulled it out, but not in time to dodge the ice ogre's punch.

The impact threw her in the air and she landed several feet away. An uprooted tree scraped her arm on her way down and she winced, biting back the sharp pain that shot up her arm. Tiny crimson drops of blood spilled from the scratch as Red staggered to her feet and turned to face the ice ogre again. When the monster charged forward, her lips curled up and adrenaline surged through her body.

Bring it on.

She threw the hood of her red cloak over her head, and the ice ogre stopped. She hadn't moved from where she'd been standing, yet the ogre looked around in confusion. Shielded from view with her invisibility cloak, she reached for an arrow. Just as Robin had taught her, she nocked the arrow on her bow and pulled back. Closing one eye to perfect her aim, she zeroed in on her target. As soon as she let go of the arrow, it became visible to the ice monster, but it was too late for him to react before it pierced him in the chest.

The frozen creature looked down briefly as if she had merely thrown a snowball at it. Then the arrow froze and became part of its monstrous body. Something happened to its face that she could swear resembled a smile. Then the ice ogre sucked in a deep breath and blew a blizzard so hard in her direction that it threw her back against a tree. Though Red was still invisible, the ice ogre cocked his head as if he could now see the outline of her cloak covered in snow. The creature charged at her again, and she dove out of his way, scraping her knee on a boulder.

She reached for another arrow, but the monster was already running in her direction with its enormous feet ready to crush her.

Then a flaming arrow came from within the trees and pierced the ice ogre on the arm. It jolted backward and groaned as the arm melted. Giant drops of white slush fell to the ground. Another flaming arrow whistled past Red, hitting the ice ogre in the eye. It wailed as its face began to melt. Once its head was gone, its body dropped to the ground with a loud thud, only to turn back into a mountain of snow.

Red swung around and spotted Will Scarlet stepping out from behind the tree with a smug smile on his face. "Hey, Red Cheeks."

She pulled the hood off her head and scowled at him. "I had it under control," she grumbled, trying to get back up. The stupid dress was stuck on a tree root, which forced her to land back on the dirt with a thump. "And it was *one* time! I hardly think it merits a nickname!"

"You mean when I caught you spying on me?"

"I was not!" She looked up at him, both angry and mortified. "How was I supposed to know you were bathing in that waterfall?"

The image of Will whipping his head back with his bare upper body under the plunging waterfall flashed before Red's mind. Thousands of glittering drops clung to his defined muscles, and a little ray of sunshine rested on his tanned body like he was a Greek god. Just the thought sent heat rushing to Red's cheeks again.

Will laughed as he stood over her. "Need a hand?"

"I got it." She untied her cloak from her neck then reached for the part of the dress that was stuck. She yanked it until it ripped and broke free. Will cleared his throat, and she looked up to find him slightly flushed. Just as she was about to ask him what was wrong, she caught his eyes stealing at glance at her chest before averting them. She looked down at her corset, which was so tight, it gave her an actual cleavage for the first time in her life.

"I'm never wearing a dress again," she grumbled as she covered her chest with her cloak.

"So, what was that all about?" Will asked, turning to look in the direction of the castle. "I thought it was Aria's coronation today?"

"Oh, it was her coronation all right." Red's expression soured, and Will frowned. "Looks like we might have another Evil Queen in our kingdom. And worse than the one prior."

"Aria?" Will's dark brows raised, but Red shook her head.

"That wasn't Aria," she said, looking at the empty balcony where Aria had been standing. It was so small and insignificant in the distance that it was hard to believe that just minutes earlier Aria sent Prince George to his death from it. "That was The Snow Queen... or whatever the heck she calls herself now."

"I just don't understand... Why? How?"

Red shook her head, her heart heavy in her chest. Her friend was gone, and she had no idea how to get her back. "We need to find Robin. If anyone can knock some sense into her, it's probably him."

"Or he'll just pierce her with an arrow," Will joked, and Red's lips lifted a little. Will's grin widened at her reaction, seeming surprised she found that funny.

Red shook her head as if shaking off a spell and looked away from his dimples. But when she looked around and didn't see his horse, she stopped. "How did you get here?"

He hesitated but only for a moment. "I

guess my horse got spooked by those ice monsters. Where's yours?"

She rolled her eyes, then put two fingers between her teeth and whistled. A moment later, her light brown horse, Scout, came galloping from within the woods.

After climbing on, she waited for Will to join her. As he mounted, Red's back pressed against Will's hot chest, prompting her cheeks to burn.

"That way is north." Will pointed to the right. "But don't go thinking you're going to rest."

She let out a tired grunt as she nudged the horse to move. "Is Robin waiting?"

"Yep."

*B*y the time they arrived at the village in Sherwood, Robin and Little John were fastening their horses' saddles outside the tavern.

"It's about time," Robin said, then did a double take at his cousin's disheveled appearance. She caught her reflection in the windows and squinted. Her face was smeared with mud while leaves hung from her brown hair. She picked the leaves out as Robin cocked a brow at her. "What happened to you?"

"The Snow Queen," Red answered as Will dismounted, and she followed. "Something happened to Aria. You need to talk to her."

Robin laughed mockingly. "I don't need to do anything for her. She protected The Intruder, remember?"

"Jack wasn't The Intruder," Red reminded him. "And Aria is our friend—"

"She left us." Robin turned around with his piercing green eyes, glaring. "Or don't you remember waking up one morning to find that she was gone? After everything we did for her."

Red frowned. "She was protecting us."

"She was protecting herself." His face twisted like he'd sucked on a lemon. "Now, we have other responsibilities to attend to, so please… go change so we can be on our way."

He turned around and continued saddling his horse. Red let out a sigh. She knew he cared for Aria, but the scars from his abandonment issues were too deep. Maybe one day he would understand that when people moved on, it wasn't *him* they were leaving behind.

Back in her room, Red stepped out of the heavy dress and ripped open the corset, grateful to take a deep breath for the first time that day. It only took her a few minutes to put on her favorite ensemble: a pair of tan cotton pants and a thick white shirt. She pulled on her leather boots, tied her hair into a braid, and went back outside, ready to go. She exchanged looks with Will before mounting her horse. He gave her a small nod as a silent query if she was ready, and she nodded back. He then darted into the woods on his horse, and Robin grinned with his dirty blond hair glistening from the sun. Little John, who was ironically anything but little, followed suit with Red behind him.

Though trotting in the back, Red could still see Will at the front. She kept her eyes on him as he maneuvered through the forest like he belonged there. Will was their best tracker. Not only did he know how to find the exact location of where the carriages would cross through, but he had such a kind and friendly face that drunken sailors at the tavern had no problem spilling information about Prince John's shipments in casual conversation.

That was how they met the man who later came to be known as The Intruder. Normally, Red wouldn't give much attention to drunk talking, but hearing that he'd come from another realm through a mirror had her intrigued. Only because her friend Aria had told her about the Mirror of Reason, and how it was her only way out of the Chanted Forest.

But The Intruder didn't talk about the mirror. Instead, he talked about the wolves that hid within the woods. That had Red even more intrigued because her grandmother was mauled by a wolf when she was twelve years old, and she'd been hunting him ever since.

Robin was more interested in the money The Intruder was offering. He wanted to hire them for a job which involved capturing Princess Marian. It was no easy task considering she was to be married to Prince John by the end of that month.

That was all Robin needed to hear. Taking yet another precious gem from Prince John was music to his ears and he gladly accepted. Red was reluctant at first. Stealing from his carriages was one thing, but kidnapping his bride was something else entirely. But when The Intruder said it was the alpha of the wolves that wanted Princess Marian, Red couldn't pass up the opportunity. Red's intention was never to let the wolf take Marian. She just wanted a reason to lure the wolf out of hiding so she could pierce his heart with an arrow once and for all.

And she probably would have succeeded had Robin not left her behind. She had never told him of her plan, but he was too observant. He most likely saw the revenge brewing in her eyes. As angry as she was at Robin for not taking her along, she couldn't blame him. The wolf had already killed their grandmother. He wasn't going to risk Red's life, too. She was, after all, the only family he had left. And he was hers.

Red's horse stopped next to Robin's, and she watched Will lift his chin ahead of them. She couldn't decide if he was sniffing the air or stretching his neck. He tended to do that whenever they stopped to rest, and Red wondered if he'd injured his neck when he fell off his horse last time. She'd been meaning to ask him, but it always slipped her mind. He seemed fine most of the time, so it was probably nothing.

It took a few hours to find the dirt road he'd apparently been looking for, but when he did, he turned around and flashed Red a proud grin. He was good at tracking, and he knew it. Red rolled her eyes, not wanting to feed his ego, but then threw the hood over her head before he could catch her smiling.

"All right, everyone in position," Robin called out, jumping from his horse onto a tree then climbing to a thick enough branch where he could position himself on his stomach. He pulled an arrow from his quiver and nocked it in his bow.

Little John kicked his horse, and it galloped to the other side of the road. Then he jumped up from the saddle and climbed a different tree. He positioned himself in the same manner. Red jumped from Scout and secured the reins before slapping her hind. Her horse took off into the woods and out of sight. And the other horses followed suit, just as they were trained to do. All it would take was a whistle and they would come back.

She crouched by a tree but didn't bother hiding. She was already invisible. Yet when her eyes landed on Will across the way, he seemed to have been looking at her. Of course he wasn't. He couldn't see her. But his gaze was so gentle in her direction, she couldn't stop watching him.

He made it even more difficult when he pulled up his sleeves and the muscles on his forearm flexed. Red wouldn't have been watching him like this had she not been invisible. If only she had been fast enough with her cloak the day she caught him bathing at the waterfall, he would never have known she was there. Of course, she wouldn't have watched him any longer, but at least he wouldn't have seen her face turn beet red.

Now, every time he called her *Red*, a flutter rose in her stomach from the memory of that day. His chiseled chest dripping wet would forever be engraved in her mind. And it didn't help that he still kept taking off his shirt around her. She hated how much of a girl he made her feel. Growing up with Robin, she was always part of the guys, and none of them ever looked at her any differently. But since

Will joined the crew, she'd suddenly begun to care about whether or not her hair had been washed.

A loud thud shook the ground as a large tree branch fell across the road. Will threw aside the ax he used to cut the branch, then climbed next to Little John, the muscles on his arms popping from the strain.

"Red, get ready." Robin's voice was soft but focused, and Red shifted her attention to the galloping hooves in the distance.

A carriage, which looked like it belonged to Prince John, slowed to a stop with two guards on it. One of the guards jumped down and held open the carriage door as a man stepped out to inspect the fallen branch. It was the despicable Prince.

Red heard the taut strings of Robin's bow creak above her, then an arrow whistled through the wind before piercing the leather straps out of the hands of one of the guards. The horses screeched, but by the time both men turned around, Will swung from the tree and kicked the guard off the carriage, taking his place. Will released both horses from their bonds then jumped on one of them, leaving the carriage behind. The Prince, as well as the guards, leapt out of the way as the horses darted in their direction.

Both guards jumped to their feet, then ran after Will with their swords drawn. Little John's arrow cut through The Prince's royal attire, pinning him to a nearby tree. Before The Prince could yank on the arrow, Little John shot him again. The Prince yelped as the second arrow grazed his leg.

Robin's arrow whistled through the wind again, then landed on the lock of the carriage, bursting the door open. "Red, go!"

Red took off toward the open door as the guards ran back with their swords raised. Their screams seemed to infuse them with courage. Not that it mattered. Even if they knew about her, they wouldn't see her.

Red jumped into the carriage and pulled open a compartment under the cushioned seat. Five velvet bags came into view, and Red swiped them all. As soon as she touched them, they disappeared just like her, and she shoved them inside her satchel under her cloak.

When she turned around, the guards had reached the carriage. "They're gone!" they called out to The Prince, who was still trying to free himself from the tree. "The jewels are gone!"

"Get them, you idiots!" The Prince yelled, the veins on his neck popping in anger. The guards swung around, their eyes roaming the woods.

Red stepped out of the carriage then walked carefully around them, trying not to make any noise. Once she stepped on the grass, she ran up the hill and whistled loudly. Wind picked up and rustled the leaves on the trees as Red listened for the responding neigh from Scout. A few tense moments passed until the sound of hooves hitting the ground drowned out her racing heart. The horses came galloping back, and Red climbed onto Scout while Robin mounted his steed. The guards charged uphill in Robin's direction, but then heard Little John behind them and stopped.

"Go!" The Prince yelled, ripping his jacket against the arrow. "Get my jewels back!"

Red urged Scout to catch up to Robin as they darted north, then pulled her hood off her head. Their eyes locked briefly, and he flashed her a smile. "Well done, partner."

She returned a smug look. "I'll race you to the tavern."

Robin's smile grew wider. "You're on."

* * *

*B*ack at the tavern at Sherwood, the young men enjoyed their drinks in the corner. Normally, Robin would buy the whole bar drinks to celebrate yet another victory, but tonight he didn't seem in the mood. Though pleased with the job well done, Red could tell he was thinking about Marian again because he picked a spot on the table and stared at it until his cup was empty.

Ever since he handed Marian over to the wolves, Robin hadn't been himself. Especially after The Intruder left pages of a story from his realm for Robin to find. Apparently, in that story, Robin and Marian were a couple madly in love. He was never supposed to have given her to the wolves. He was supposed to have *saved* her from The Prince and married her instead.

"Rumor has it The Intruder has gone back to his realm," he finally muttered, looking up at Will who sat across from him. "Our only shot at finding Marian is to find the wolves. Maybe they took her to their lair or something."

"Their *lair?*" Red echoed teasingly. "This isn't a king cobra we're dealing with."

The corners of Will's mouth lifted a little before he put on a serious face with a cough, covering up his amusement. Robin took another swig of his drink. "Then what is your theory?" he asked, turning to his cousin.

"We don't even know if she's still alive—"

"I know she is," Robin said curtly before finishing the rest of his beer. She wasn't used to seeing the emotional side of her cousin. Normally he was the logical one, but when it came to Marian, he'd become quite driven by his heart. And all because of some pages from a book that apparently told his story with Marian had The Intruder never messed with their fate.

"Robin is right," Will said, and Red looked at him across the table. "If the wolves only wanted a woman to kill, they wouldn't have gone through all the trouble of getting The Intruder to hire Robin to kidnap Marian. They would have hunted a random stranger from one of the villages and called it a day."

"I know you like to be optimistic, but these are wild beasts we're talking about," Red replied, a lot more forcefully than she'd intended. "What if there's some sort of sick thrill of the chase or something? We don't know how these creatures think."

Little John came to join them at the table, bringing with him a bowl of broth and a plate of crusty bread. Red sighed as her stomach rumbled. She could always count on Little John to show up with food at just the right time. He was also an excellent cook. Robin and Red grabbed a piece, but she noticed Will didn't. He was staring into his mug with his brows furrowed.

"Anything?" Robin asked Little John, his eyes wide and eager.

Little John sat next to Will and leaned in, lowering his voice. "The man behind the bar said he's heard of some sightings to the south. No one mentioned a woman, but there have been killings."

"Killings?" Will turned to Little John, intrigued.

"Animals have been found slaughtered all over the forest," Little John repeated what the bartender had told him. "According to what he's heard, the bite marks resemble that of dinosaurs."

Will's expression softened, and he chuckled.

"What?" Little John asked.

"Dinosaurs, really?'

Little John shrugged then returned to his bowl. "He said it, not me."

Stories in the tavern came mostly from drunken sailors who, time and again, swore to have seen the Loch Ness Monster. So, there was no limit to their exaggerations.

"What if we found a wolf hunter?" Red suggested. "They know how to find wolves— and even capture them."

"They also charge the kind of money we don't have," Robin added. "We don't need them. Will's a tracker, and we are more than capable of catching them on our own. We just need to keep trying."

"Well, I think a good night's rest will do us

good," Will said, chugging down his drink then placing the empty cup on the center of the table. "How about we revisit the topic in the morning when we're not so exhausted?"

"Spoken like the true voice of reason," Red agreed with Will, but she also knew it would take quite a few more drinks to knock Robin down to a snoring sleep. She watched as Will stood and walked out of the tavern and into the freezing blizzard.

When the door slammed shut from the wind, the icy chill invaded the tavern, and Red shivered. She wrapped her cloak around her body then turned to her cousin.

"Robin, we need to do something about Aria."

"Don't worry about her." He waved it off. "The Evil Queen put the poor girl through a tortuous year. She's probably just letting off some steam. She'll come around. I'm sure."

"She threw a friend into the lake and froze it over."

Robin shrugged. "He probably had it coming."

Red let out a frustrated breath. It was hard to have a serious conversation when he was in this mood—where he was so focused on one thing that people could tell him the sky was falling and he'd shrug it off with a jest. When Robin ordered another round, Red knew it wouldn't be long before he started blabbering about Marian again.

"She's perfect, Red," Robin mumbled. "Absolutely perfect."

"And how do you know that she'll be exactly like the story The Intruder gave you?" Red asked, and Robin pulled the folded papers from his jacket.

"This describes *me* exactly how I am," he said. "So, I'm certain it describes her just as accurately."

It wouldn't do any good to argue with him. He wouldn't even remember half of that conversation in the morning, anyway. "May true love prevail then," she said in a teasing tone, but Robin's face remained serious, and he grabbed her hand.

"Thank you, Red." He gave it a tight squeeze. "I know this whole thing is a long shot and dangerous, so thank you for sticking by me."

"Of course," she said, offering him a smile. "That's what family's for."

What she didn't tell him, however, was that her motivation wasn't entirely selfless. Red made it her personal vendetta to catch the alpha. And when she did... his fate would be worse than death.

CHAPTER 2

Will stepped out of the tavern and bowed his head against the roaring blizzard. The sky grew dark with black clouds while snow battered the ground. It was as if the heavens were angry. His ears picked up the distant roars of the ice ogres roaming the forest, but Will diverted his attention away from the sound and sniffed the air.

Every now and then he caught a waft of something familiar, but then it faded before he could work out what or who it was. Red's floral scent flooded his nostrils, mingled with Robin and Little John's earthy aromas. He shook his head and walked farther into the forest.

Under the protection of the trees, the storm quieted as if a blanket had been draped over the treetops. Will's senses sharpened and he sucked in a breath, happy to be out of the blizzard. An owl hooted, possibly a mile to the north. The rustle of leaves and pitter-patter of tiny feet took over Will's attention. His stomach groaned. He should have grabbed a bite at the tavern, but Robin and Red were talking about wolves like they were cold-blooded killers. So, even though it had been days since he'd had a decent meal, he had lost his appetite.

He sniffed the air around him. There was no human nearby. He marched over to a bush and removed his sheepskin jacket. The cool air nipped at his skin, the hairs on his arms standing on end as he pulled off his shirt. He finished undressing and folded up his clothes in a pile and hid them inside the bush, out of sight.

Once bare, his defined muscles tensed as he sensed every molecule of his body trembling. A jet of fire burned through his core and his body transformed. A cloak of brown fur covered every inch of him, and he leapt into the air, landing on four padded paws. He arched his back and howled.

It felt so good to be back in wolf form. His senses sharpened tenfold. From the tiny grains of dirt beneath his sensitive paws, to the rustle and snap as a squirrel scaled a tree at least ten miles away. As he sprinted through the forest, Will kept his mind focused on getting a message out with his thoughts. The connection with his pack used to be so strong, and he missed having the constant chatter in his mind. But so much had changed.

I need to talk to you.

He set his jaw and closed his eyes. A very faint whisper entered his mind, but it was not strong enough to make out the words. His ears shot up and he turned his head in the direction of a peculiar sound. A squeal of a door hinge, and the thud of a tankard hitting the stone table in the tavern. The scratching of claws as a mouse scurried along the wooden floorboards.

A soft laugh flooded his ears and his chest squeezed. Red had chuckled at one of Little John's bad jokes. He turned back and launched into a sprint. His legs bent and bounded along the dirt path at an impossible speed. The wintery cold air could no longer touch his skin, yet it rippled through his fur, sending a shiver of delight. He howled again, this time in a playful way, and ran as fast as his limbs would allow.

The familiar scent came back, and Will stopped.

Please, I really need to talk to you.

The whisper returned, this time louder than before, and Will inwardly sighed with relief at knowing he'd been heard.

I hear you. The voice entered his mind sounded like his own, but Will knew it was Levi's.

Levi, it's so good to hear from you. Will settled down on his belly and rested his head on his front paws as he dragged his tail side to side. But Levi did not sound equally happy to hear from him.

I shouldn't be talking to you, Levi said. *After what you did, the alpha has forbidden it.*

Will puffed air out of his nostrils and then grumbled under his breath.

Has the alpha still got Marian?

Yes.

What does he want with her?

Levi hesitated, but only for a moment. *Revenge.*

How do I find her?

Levi didn't respond, and for a moment Will wondered if his question was a step too far. To give away that information would have been a betrayal. He felt bad for putting him in that position. Levi was a young wolf with a good heart. But Will needed answers.

You'll pick up a trail if you carry on east, Levi finally answered.

It wasn't much to go on, but it was enough. Will jumped to his feet and howled again. He thanked Levi, but he was already gone. His mind was empty and quiet once more. Then his ears pricked up at the sound of a girl's scream.

He broke into a sprint and raced through the woods, baring his teeth. Dark clouds covered the moonlight, but Will's wolf eyes were sharper than when he was in human form. His nose guided him as he followed the sickly-sweet aroma of berries mingled with the metallic taste of blood. He puffed as his paws padded the crunchy snow, and even when his ears picked up an entirely new sound, he didn't slow down his pace.

He leapt over a riverbank, landing perfectly on the other side.

"Help me!" A young girl's scream was like nails dragging along a chalkboard, and a guttural growl escaped Will's throat. The unearthly roar flooded his ears again as he rounded a corner. He darted through the trees until his eyes made out the silhouette of a little girl.

She could not have been older than ten, her blonde hair tied in bunches and she wore a small green cloak. Her little eyes were like two tiny moons, looking up at her attacker. Without thinking, Will bounded into the clearing just as a giant white bear threw its paw out to strike.

Will took the full force of the blow and whimpered as his body struck a nearby tree. He jumped up and shook it off, trying to dissolve the deep ache in his back. Adrenaline coursed through his veins and he caught sight of the little girl dropping a bag of berries and running back toward the village. He turned back to the white bear and growled again.

It soon became clear that this being was not an animal. There was nothing behind its frozen eyes, and as it struck him again, he realized its paw was solid. The bear was made entirely of ice. Will got up and circled the bear. Its eyes remained focused on him. Will bared his fangs and raised up on his back feet, clawing the air to get the bear to back down.

Any animal would either take on the fight or back away in submission. But this creature merely opened its mouth and roared again. Frozen snowflakes spewed out of its mouth, and Will snorted as they tickled his nose. He shook his head to find his bearings and bent down, ready to pounce.

The bear grunted and slammed Will's head with its icy paw, pinning him to the ground and sending a jolt of pain to Will's head. It felt like the worst brain freeze of his life. He squirmed and whimpered, but the bear's paw only pressed harder.

He curled his lips back, baring his teeth again. He snapped and rolled out of the bear's hold and launched onto its back. The fur melted under his paws and he struggled to keep his balance. This was definitely not an animal. He gnashed his teeth and bit into the bear's neck, wrestling it to the ground. Taking all of his energy, he tore off an icy chunk of the bear's neck and spat it out. The strange creature did not cry out in pain, but instead fell to the ground, collapsing in a pile of powdered snow.

Will panted for several minutes to regain his strength, then his mind returned to the little girl. He sniffed the air and picked up her trail. He bounded to the tree where he'd hidden his clothes and closed his eyes, relaxing his muscles and allowing his body to transform back into human form.

The pain reached new heights as he staggered on his two legs and shakily put on his clothes. He stumbled forward, the blizzard air hitting his body like ice daggers but melting against his burning skin. The cold was oddly numbing and a welcome relief from his wounds.

Now dressed, he sprinted and caught up with the small girl as she hid behind a tree, winded and silently crying. As the clouds parted and the silvery moonlight shone over them, Will noticed the fear in her wet eyes as she looked up at him.

"Please, don't hurt me," she whimpered, her small body trembling.

Will raised his hands in an unthreatening manner as he approached. "I won't hurt you. I'm from Sherwood Forest, just like you," he said softly.

The girl bit her lip as giant tears rolled down her cheeks. "My momma told me not to go into the forest, but I'm so hungry."

Will handed her the fallen berries which he'd scooped up on his way. "Here. I'm sorry it's not much."

"Thank you," the little girl said in a breathy voice as she clutched the berries in her little hands.

Will's heart wrenched. He wished he had more food to give. The pale color of her face and hollow eyes made him wonder how long it had been since she last ate. It was bad enough that The Evil Queen had burned several villages to the ground, causing the food trade to take a hit. Now, since The Snow Queen rose to power, it unleashed an eternal winter over the kingdom. If something wasn't done soon, there would be no people left to rule.

He shook the thoughts from his mind. He needed to focus on one task at a time. He stood and watched the little girl run back into the village, listening to her creep back into her home. The door lock clicked, and he exhaled the breath he had been holding. Knowing she was finally safe, he walked back to the tavern.

Most patrons had retired, and Robin was nowhere in sight. Yet his scent lingered, so he knew he was still close by. Little John and Red were still sitting at the table, chatting.

"Where have you been?" Little John asked, his bushy brows raised. He held a plate of left-over bread and Will took a piece and stuffed it in his mouth.

"Making myself useful," he said between bites. "I've got us a lead."

Red jumped up from the table and hurried over to him with wide eyes. "You know where the wolf is?" she asked excitedly.

Will smirked, happy to see the admiration in her eyes. To her, he had achieved the impossible. "Get your rest. We're riding east in the morning."

CHAPTER 3

Weak morning sunlight peeked through the thick clouds as Red galloped ahead to ride beside Will, while Robin and Little John followed behind. Little John talked about the times when Aria used to be part of their group. Red's heart squeezed in her chest. She missed her friend. Whoever that Snow Queen was, that wasn't her friend.

Aria was kind and brave, but never evil. Robin took her under his wing after she fled from her home and The Evil Queen. Robin wasn't one to have pity for people, but he saw great potential in Aria, just as he'd seen in Red. And he'd treated Aria like family.

It was nice having another girl around.

Especially after Red's grandmother died, and she went to live with Robin. She'd been the only girl around the men for years, so Aria became the sister Red never had. They were a lot alike in the way they quickly learned how to fight with a sword and shoot an arrow, but they were also different in how they grieved the loss of their family.

Aria spent a whole year running away and hiding from The Queen who'd killed her family. Red, on the other hand, spent most of her life waiting for the day she would come face to face with her grandmother's killer.

Her memory of that day was still so vivid in her mind. She could still hear her grandmother's scream echo in the forest... the ache in her legs as she ran back home... the creak of the wooden door as she pushed it open... the copper smell of blood when she walked in. Her Grams was on the floor, exhaling her last breath, and that was when Red heard it. The howl of the wolf—the killer—in the distance as if it were taunting her, challenging her.

She should've gone after him. Hunted him. Killed him. But she didn't know any better at the age of twelve. So, she did what any other child would do—mounted her horse and rushed to find the only other family she had. Robin.

Red wasn't twelve anymore. Now that she knew how to fight and defend herself, she was ready to face her ultimate enemy and take his life once and for all. She only ever told Aria that. They'd even talked about going after the wolf together, but when The Queen found out they'd been hiding Aria and burnt down their village, Red's priorities shifted. They needed money to rebuild the village, which meant more *jobs* with Robin.

Still, the anchor of revenge weighed heavy on her heart with each passing day, and the anger for the wolf only grew stronger with time.

"So intense." Will's voice snapped her out of her thoughts.

She glanced at him, unsure if she'd missed something he'd said.

"There's that intense look you get when you're thinking really hard." He furrowed his brows in a poor imitation of her expression, and she chuckled despite her heavy heart.

"I look that bad, huh?"

"Not *that* bad," he teased. "So, what's got you so serious?"

"My Grams." She flashed him a soft smile, hoping it would mask the sadness that still came with the memory. "It's been six years."

Will didn't respond. He knew how her grandmother had died, and even though Red was trying hard not to make the conversation take a depressing turn, she knew he was too sensitive to ignore her pain.

"You know," he finally said after a few moments, "I didn't know her, but I think she would've been proud of the woman you've become."

"And who is that?" Red wasn't even sure of the answer herself, so it piqued her curiosity to know what Will would say.

"You're strong and brave in front of everyone," he said, keeping his eyes on the road. "And you don't hesitate to fight for your people, even if it means risking your own life."

"But?" she asked, noticing the crease between his brows.

"But the girl hidden under that cloak has weaknesses and fears just like everyone else."

He turned and their eyes met. "That girl... isn't invisible to me."

The gentleness in his eyes had always filled her with calm, and today was no exception.

"How much farther?" Robin called out from behind, jolting them into ripping their gaze away from each other.

Will focused on the road again. "Just over that hill," he called back.

Robin kicked his horse to gallop ahead, and Little John followed. Red rolled her eyes, and Will smiled. He then gave her a nod, waiting for her to go ahead of him. By the time she caught up to Robin and Little John with Will behind her, they had stopped by a ravine. Red jumped down from Scout and peered over the edge with her heart in her mouth. Her boot scuffed the rocky ground and a piece of gravel tumbled over the edge, falling like a raindrop to the bottom. They were so high up, she never heard it hit the ground.

"Now what?" Will asked, turning to Robin.

Robin looked around. "We'll need to cross over on foot," he said, looking at a thin wooden bridge a few feet away. Frayed rope held the bridge together and it swayed side to side, creaking in the wind.

"Is that even safe?" Little John asked, looking at the bridge with fear in his eyes. Red wasn't surprised. It didn't take much to scare Little John. But in this case, he wasn't wrong. The bridge was too narrow for the horses and the planks were covered with snow. If any of the wood was rotten, they wouldn't be able to see it.

Robin jumped down from his horse and tightened the strap on his quiver. "What are you waiting for?" He slapped Little John's leg as he walked past. "Let's go."

Red watched Robin while Will dismounted, sheathing his knife. When his eyes locked with hers, there was a hint of worry in his expression. But had his concern been with the instability of the bridge or Robin's blind determination, Red wasn't sure.

Jumping down from Scout, she secured her horse to a nearby tree then nuzzled her snout, puffing air to Scout's nose. "I'll be back," she whispered.

"I think it'll hold," Robin said, grabbing

the rope on each side and yanking it to make sure it was firm before stepping onto the snow-covered plank. "Seems sturdy enough."

Not very reassuring, but Red followed with Will close behind her. As she stepped onto the bridge, she realized it wasn't as bad as she had feared. But then Robin slipped and let out a panicked cry.

"Robin!" She grabbed his shirt with shaking hands as his foot dangled over the edge. His shoulders trembled against her firm grip, and it took her a few seconds for her to realize he was laughing.

"Are you serious?" Her blood boiled and she slapped him on the head. "That is not funny at all!"

He pulled himself back up, still laughing. "Oh, come on. That was a little funny."

"You have a twisted sense of humor," she muttered, fighting the urge to slap him again.

Will's chest pressed against her stiff back. "Just don't look down and you'll be fine."

She nodded, feeling his warmth through the fabric of her clothes. As she took another step forward, an icy chill blew through them, making even Robin shiver. But then he halted, forcing the group to come to an abrupt stop.

"What's wrong?" Red asked.

"Take a wild guess," Robin replied through gritted teeth.

"Hi there, old friend." Aria stood at the other end of the bridge, her white-blonde hair flowed freely in the breeze. A long fur-lined cloak adorned her narrow frame as she pulled off her leather gloves with elegance and poise. She touched the rope, and when it turned to ice, her lips lifted a little. "You're a very hard man to find, Robin."

"What can I say…" Robin tried to sound relaxed, but Red could tell by the tension still in his shoulders that he couldn't wait to get to safer grounds. "I've been busy trying to find food for my people since *The Snow Queen* decided to curse the kingdom with the harshest of winters."

"It wasn't me…" She stopped herself, and for a flicker of a second Red saw a resemblance of her friend. But then Aria's expression hardened again. "On second thought, it doesn't matter. I'm not here to chitchat."

"Then why are you here?"

"Contrary to what you might think, I do want you to find Marian."

Robin let out a laugh. "Is that right?"

"Can we finish this conversation once we've crossed the bridge?" Red chimed in, but Aria raised a hand.

"Not so fast."

"What do you want, Aria?" Robin asked with an impatient edge in his tone.

"I want the pages of your story."

Red couldn't see her cousin's face, but his hand gripped the rope as if he were balling his fists. "What for?"

"I'm afraid that doesn't concern you." She reached out her hand. "Now, hand them over."

Robin steeled himself, grabbing onto the rope with an even firmer grip. "No."

Aria's lips lifted into a wicked grin. "I don't think you understand what you're bargaining here." She waved her hand in the air and the bridge turned to ice.

Robin recoiled from the frozen rope, as did Red. Will touched her arms, steadying her as the wood became slippery.

Little John let out a panicked screech, and

Red whipped around. He was slipping off the edge and Will jumped, catching his arm just as he slid off the side. Red dropped to her knees and grabbed Will's shirt to stop him from sliding.

"Aria!" Red glanced over her shoulder at her friend, and for a split second she saw Aria frown. "He's going to fall!"

Aria looked at Robin. "The pages."

Robin grunted as he reached into his quiver. After he pulled out the pages, he held them up. "Let us through."

Aria stepped back, stretching out both hands in front of her and expanding the narrow bridge into a wide and solid plank made of ice. Will pulled John back up, and Red let out a relieved breath.

Robin marched toward Aria with a scowl, but that didn't seem to intimidate her. She crossed her arms and waited until he stomped in front of her.

"Remember when I said you have what it takes to be a ruler?" Robin hissed. "I couldn't have been more wrong."

Aria's jaw clenched, as did her fists. "You have *no* idea what it takes to be a ruler." Her voice came out as a growl as she stepped toward him. "Now, hand over the pages before I turn you into a sculpture of ice."

Robin handed over the folded papers, and Aria snatched it from his hand. While she scanned through them to make sure they were the correct ones, Red dropped on the ground next to Robin, as did Will and Little John.

"What's happened to you?" Robin asked as if he didn't recognize the young woman he'd once taken under his wing.

Aria's eyes saddened. "Responsibility." She shoved the pages into her satchel then whistled. A winged horse made of ice appeared from thin air and landed on the edge of the cliff. She climbed on its back, then turned to look at Robin again. "Tip to the wise. I wouldn't keep going in that direction if I were you."

"And why would I listen to you?" he responded.

"Because you're headed toward the Ice Mountains," she said. "That's the last place the wolves would go."

"What do you know about the wolves?" Red asked, jumping to her feet.

Aria's eyes softened for a moment. "You're still determined to catch the alpha for what he did to your grandmother, aren't you?"

Red didn't have to answer, her glare and clenched fists said enough.

"Your best shot will be using a black arrow," Aria said. "Do you remember how to make one?"

Red nodded, ignoring Will's concerned eyes on her.

"Until we meet again, my friend." Aria's ice horse lifted from the ground, flapping its wings, blowing an icy wind in their direction.

Once Aria disappeared, Robin turned to Red. "What the heck is a black arrow?"

"Let's go home, Robin." Red headed toward the ice bridge, but Robin didn't follow.

"Not yet."

Red turned around with a puzzled look. "Did you not hear what Aria said? We've been going in the wrong direction."

"I don't believe her."

"I think she was telling the truth," Will chimed in, only to get a frown from Robin. "I'm just saying, the wolves wouldn't go anywhere near the mountain men."

Robin narrowed his eyes. "How would you know what the wolves wouldn't do?"

Will's face hardened. "I don't."

"Then we keep going." Robin turned his back on them and headed into the woods. Little John followed, leaving Red and Will behind.

"Who are the mountain men?" Red asked in a whisper.

"I'm not sure," Will replied, his eyes locked on Robin's back as he walked deeper into the forest. "But I have a feeling we're going to find out."

CHAPTER 4

"I don't like this… I really don't like this," Little John muttered as they walked. Frozen leaves crunched beneath their boots, and everyone kept their head bowed against the howling wind. Everyone except Will. His body ran at a higher temperature than the average human. And with his increased sense of hearing, he suspected he was the only one who could hear Little John's incessant murmurs.

"We should go back," Little John said in a shaky voice. "This is foolhardy."

Will wasn't scared nearly as often as Little John, but, to his credit, Little John could pick a lock faster than anyone. However, in this scenario, there were no locks to pick. Only snow and trees.

As the forest thickened, Robin drew his sword and swung it hard, cutting through the undergrowth as he led the group forward. Will picked up the rear, walking behind Red, listening out for the slightest sound of an enemy. But any sounds were drowned out by Red's teeth chattering.

Will removed his cloak and wrapped it around her small shoulders.

"Aren't you cold?" she asked, arching a brow. Still, she didn't argue. Her pretty lips had turned blue, and she wrapped the cloak around her like a blanket. "How is your cloak so warm?"

Will smiled at her but then looked ahead before she caught him staring.

"Robin, Little John is right," Red said. "We should go back."

"And the sky is growing dark," Will added, but Robin didn't answer. Will sighed and shared a look with Red.

"Stubborn as a mule, that one," she murmured under her breath. Will snorted.

"Robin, it's too cold to keep going." Little

John stopped and leaned against an ice-covered tree trunk. He bent over his knees, huffing with deep, ragged breaths. Will could even hear his heart racing.

Robin walked back and put a hand on Little John's tired shoulder. "Okay, fine." He didn't seem happy about it, but he wasn't going to push any of them past their limit. They were all malnourished from the lack of food. If it weren't for Will hunting as a wolf, he would've been just as weak. "We'll set up camp here tonight."

Will's eyes locked on the tree behind Little John. Something was off, as if the tree had moved somehow. "Robin…" Will frowned and took a step closer. "What's that?"

Red stood shivering next to Will and turned with her brows furrowed. Robin swung around. At first glance, it appeared that the white tree shifted, but then Will's eyes narrowed on the steely face of a tall man painted white. Robin jumped back, pulling Little John with him.

"What in the world?" Little John rubbed his backside as he shuffled to a stand. A camouflaged man stepped away from the tree trunk. Though he stood head and shoulders taller than everyone, his body was painted in icy blue and white with markings that camouflaged perfectly with the frozen wood grain.

The man growled. The sound was unlike anything Will had heard before. A guttural howl came from deeper into the forest, and for the first time, Will had goosebumps. Another man stepped out from the hedge growth.

Icy whispers flew around, sending shivers up Will's spine. They were surrounded.

Will tensed and looked down in time to see Red lift her hood, disappearing from view. Little John grounded his footing and pulled out his knife, as did Will. There was a collective sniff followed by more growling. It was as if these men were savages in their own way. But there was a harsh, coldness about them. They were unnatural, with the most offensive odor emitting from their painted flesh. These unearthly creatures could only be the mountain men.

Will longed to shift and tear them all to shreds. But transforming now would mean revealing the truth about himself, not only to Robin and Little John, but to Red. And if that happened, he was sure to lose the only family he'd had since his brother died. And Red... he couldn't even bear the thought of how much it would hurt her. Yet, if he snuck away, it wouldn't go unnoticed.

No, this confrontation had to be done in human form.

In a swift move, Robin secured an arrow in his bow and scowled as he released it. The arrow defied the laws of physics as it flew in a perfectly straight line through the blizzard. It landed right in between the mountain man's eyes, but instead of piercing his skin, the arrow shattered—splinters falling to the ground as if the arrow had been put through a wood chipper.

Impenetrable skin? No wonder the wolves were afraid of these creatures.

Leaves rustled next to Will, and his eyes narrowed at the footprints appearing in the snow. But no visible person made them. A second later, the mountain men's knife disappeared from his waist, and immediately Will knew Red had touched it while in her invisible form. The mountain man flickered his eyes to the invisible weapon, then stretched forth a hand and curled his fingers around something, as if holding a dead turkey by its neck. Will couldn't see Red, but he could hear her choking.

"Let her go!" Little John swung his sword, but the man caught it between his fingers and his upper lip curled, revealing sharp, pointed teeth. Will kicked the snowy ground with so much force, a shower of ice and twigs flew in the man's eyes. The mountain man dropped his hand and wiped his face with a grunt, giving Will just enough time to grasp Red's hand. She stumbled to the ground and her hood fell from her head. She reappeared, panting and clutching her throat.

Little John swung his sword again at the mountain men's arm as he tried to recapture Red. The blade bent upon impact, but it still kept the creature from grasping his target. Robin grabbed Little John and pulled him to start running, but then he stopped and pulled out another arrow just as two more mountain men appeared. Will's brain raced as he urged Red to run faster back toward the bridge. He didn't know anything about these creatures, but that was his fault. If only he'd been as studious as his sister, Belle. She had read and studied about all of the beings living in these forests.

While running behind Little John, Robin grabbed a match and struck it against a nearby branch, lighting his arrow.

"No one touches my family," he hissed triumphantly as he drew the arrow back. As he released it, a flame shot across the space above their heads like a shooting star, then landed on the tree above the mountain man. The arrow's head pierced into the trunk, setting it ablaze. Robin wasted no time in repeating the process, and within seconds, three more flaming arrows struck the trees around them. Thick, black smoke filled the air.

"Run!" Will shouted, still dragging Red with him. Little John wasn't too far behind. He sprinted to keep up while Robin staggered, nocking another flaming arrow in his bow.

"Take the others back, I'll hold these creatures off!" Robin yelled. And that was when Will officially decided he was an idiot.

There was no holding mountain men *off*, but there was also no time to argue. Will hurried down the path, ducking under branches and trying not to pay attention to the growing number of new sounds. The hairs on the back of his neck stood on end and his nose twitched at the pungent smell of the mountain men as they closed in on them. Will didn't need to see them to know they were surrounded.

They broke free from the forest, finally returning to the ice bridge. A black cloud rolled across the sky as Robin emerged from the dark forest. He lit another match, and it illuminated the sour look on his face as he set his arrow alight.

"This is my last one," he warned before launching it into the air. No one waited for it to land. They scrambled across the bridge, running as fast as their legs would push. Even Will, in his human form, had his limitations.

They were about halfway across the bridge when the ice began to crack beneath their feet. Will glanced at the drop. The rocky cliffs were joined by a river that looked like a tiny string of water from such a height. If the bridge collapsed, there would be no hope of survival. But if they turned back, the mountain men would surely capture them.

"The bridge isn't going to hold," Will shouted, urging both Little John and Robin to hurry. Will increased his strides and pulled Red with him until they reached the other side. Red stumbled on the snow while Will swung around. Little John and Robin had stopped in their tracks, afraid the slightest movement would shatter the ice beneath them. Will stepped back on the bridge to offer help, but the piercing sound of splitting ice under his weight forced him to retreat.

"Don't move," Robin demanded, standing next to Little John. "On the count of three."

The ice continued to split, and Will stepped back, ready to shift if he had to.

"Three!" Robin took off on a sprint, grabbing Little John with him. The two of them jumped just as the bridge crumbled, and Will grabbed Little John in the air. They landed with a thump and a groan next to Red.

"Robin!" Red cried out, and Will's stomach plummeted as he sat up to find that Robin was nowhere in sight. He stared in shock into the thick haze, unable to breathe.

"No!" Red's screech clawed against Will's sensitive ears. He bolted forward and fell to his knees, leaning over the edge. But even with his enhanced vision, he couldn't make anything out through the blizzard. The winter storm picked up with ferocity, and it seemed like the earth had awoken with a roar. A thunderous current of wind and snow blasted to the sky, throwing Will off balance. He shuffled back and grabbed Red, pulling her into his chest with his arms enveloping her body.

He buried his face in her damp hair and shut his eyes, rocking her back and forth. The wind pummeled his body and he held her tighter, as if trying to keep her from falling apart. Little John sat deathly still.

"I'm so sorry," Will murmured to a shaken Red.

But before she could answer, Little John gasped. "Look!"

Will lifted his head and squinted through the storm to see a dark figure hovering in the air. Small cyclones encircled his body as if they were fashioned to keep him from falling. It drew closer, then lowered the figure to the ground.

The winds and snow evaporated, and for the first time since the coronation, the sky cleared enough for the warm sunshine to break through the clouds, illuminating the figure.

Robin!

He stood with his quiver in one hand and a sword in the other, not even a scrape on his body.

Red pulled away from Will and looked up at her cousin. Her breath hitched as she scrambled to her feet and raced into his arms. "You idiot! You stubborn, pig-headed idiot!" She alternated between giving him hugs and slapping his arm. Robin's expression darkened as his eyes shot sideways.

"You've got to be kidding…" Robin said with a grumble. "*You* saved me?"

"Who are you talking to—" Red turned to see whom Robin was staring at. A tall, young man with white hair and piercing blue eyes stood quietly, as if he had been secretly monitoring the situation from the sidelines.

Will sniffed. He could smell the metallic blood running through the young man's veins and hear his heart beating steadily. But there was something distinctly different about him. A roar rose inside the man's chest, as if the winter storm was an extension of his soul.

"Jack, what are you doing here?" Red asked.

Will watched as she took a hesitant step toward Jack, perhaps considering giving him a hug but changing her mind.

Will had only seen Jack once. They'd saved him and Aria from the ogres one night, then took them back to the village. But by morning, when Will came back from hunting, Jack and Aria had already left. The Jack from that night was different from the supernatural human standing before him now.

"This was all a trap, wasn't it?" Robin said acidly, staring at Jack with so much intensity, Will wondered if looks could actually kill.

Jack sighed and stepped forward, the air swirling mystically around him. His long silver cloak had gold stitching, and he carried a leather satchel that sported The Queen's coat of arms.

"If it were a trap..." Jack replied. "Why would I have saved your life?"

"Aria set us up," Robin spat. "We just saw her."

Jack's face fell. "She was here?" he asked. "She must've been trying to find me."

Red finally stepped forward. "Why would she be looking for you?"

Jack eyed her carefully. "To try and stop me."

"From what?" Robin asked, his eyes narrowed in suspicion. Jack didn't reply but looked ahead with a nod. Now that the storm had cleared, the other side of the ravine was visible. A line of mountain men stood, like guards, staring at them with soulless eyes.

"You're going to the Ice Mountains?" Red asked, connecting the dots. Will looked back at Jack just in time to see him nod.

"We barely made it out alive," Little John added. "What could you possibly want from those... creatures."

Jack smiled. "They won't harm me," he said, walking to the edge of the ravine. He placed a hand on Robin's shoulder. "A life for a life. Now, we're even."

Robin shrugged away with a scowl. "Listen, I don't know what game you and Aria are playing, but—"

"No games," Jack corrected. "Aria is... still Aria. She'll come around. In the meantime, I need to find my people."

"Can you at least tell her to ease up on the harsh winter?" Red pleaded. "It's been one blizzard after another since she became The Snow Queen."

"The weather isn't her fault. It's mine," Jack admitted. "I can't fully control my powers, and until I do, I fear things will only get worse. That is why I must find my ancestors in the Ice Mountains."

"Then take us with you," Robin demanded.

"Marian is not there," Jack said gently, forcing Robin's scowl to return.

"How can you be sure of that?"

"You've seen the mountain men," he said. "She wouldn't survive up there."

Robin turned to Will, the scowl still etched in his expression. "Why did we even come here then?"

Will didn't respond. Mostly because he wasn't sure of the answer himself. Why did

Levi send him in the wrong direction? Into danger?

I'm sorry, Will.

Levi's voice entered his mind.

The alpha wanted me to mislead you.

Will sniffed the air, picking up Levi's familiar scent. But it was faint. He must have been more than ten miles away.

"I'm sorry, Robin," Will said finally, his shoulders slumping with defeat. "The trail went cold."

Robin pinched the bridge of his nose and closed his eyes with a huff. "All right, Jack. Tell me what you know—" Robin turned, but Jack was gone. "Great, now we're back to square one."

"It's not Will's fault," Red said firmly.

"It doesn't matter whose fault it is. We failed." Robin slammed his fist against a tree, and flurries of snow fell to the ground. "Again."

"We're going to find her," Will assured him.

"We better," Robin said gruffly. "If it's the last thing I do."

CHAPTER 5

Back at their neighboring village, the market buzzed with people buying and selling. There must have been fifty tents set up in the square. Red gave Will his cloak back. He threw the hood over his head and hid his face, just in case they ran into some of The Prince's guards. Or the Sheriff of Nottingham. It happened more often than they cared to admit.

Little John didn't bother since his face was mostly covered with a beard, and he blended well with the crowd. Robin, on the other hand, was just plain arrogant. Hiding wasn't his style, and he wasn't afraid of anyone. It helped that the evening sky had a gloomy overcast, and Red walked around the barracks. Where normally there would be fruits and vegetables, plants and garments were being sold instead. Food was also scarce in that village, and a cut of red meat fared for more coins than a silver chalice.

Something caught Red's eye, and she stopped in front of a booth. A plant as dark as charcoal rested in a vase in the corner, and she reached to touch it.

"Careful," an older woman behind the booth said with her brows arched. "That's a very rare plant."

Red nodded. She knew exactly what kind of plant that was, and what it could be used for. "Is this all you have?" she asked, looking at the woman.

She came to stand closer to Red. "Depends," she said, lowering her voice. "What do you want it for?"

"I need to extract its liquid."

The woman arched a brow in surprise. "In that case, you will need a lot more than what I have."

Red looked at the adronna plant again. There was only enough there to coat the tip of two arrows with the extract that Aria had shown her. The black arrow she reminded Red about earlier—this was it. All she had to do was boil the plant and coat the tip of her arrow with the black goo. A simple graze from that extract, and it would be enough to paralyze the alpha.

"I'll take it," Red said, turning to the woman. "However many you have."

The woman smiled. "Those are quite expensive, dear—"

Red opened her bag and pulled out a hand full of jewels. The woman's eyes widened in surprise.

"My apologies." The woman curtsied as if Red was a princess in disguise. Red would've clarified, but the number of jewels she had in her bag would've revealed her to be a thief.

"Can you store it inside a glass for me?" Red asked, handing the woman a diamond necklace.

"Right away."

After shoving the glass jar inside her

satchel, Red went to look for the boys. It wasn't long before she found Will and Robin leaning against a rocky wall by an alley.

"Any luck finding food?" she asked.

Will glanced over his shoulder. Red followed his gaze to a rusted wooden carriage attached to a single horse. A burly man carried cases of fruits and vegetables from the carriage and stacked them against a brick wall. "Wait, you're not thinking of…?"

"Don't start," Robin grumbled.

"We can't just steal their food."

"Oh, so stealing jewels is okay?"

She scowled at him. "Stealing from people that have nothing is different."

"We're not stealing from the people," Robin hissed in a low tone. "That carriage of food is being taken to Prince John's palace. Apparently he's having a ball soon."

"Even so..." She held up her bag of jewels. "We have enough money to *buy* it. Why do we always have to steal?"

Robin shook his head as he leaned against the wall again. "I know this isn't the life you wanted, Red. But it's the life you got. And I refuse to give any more money to that despicable prince."

Before Red could respond, Will tensed next to her. She followed his gaze again toward the alley and spotted Little John jumping from a low roof onto a horse of the carriage. The burly man yelled after him as he kick-started the animal and the food-laden carriage began to roll forward. Robin ran alongside it as it passed them, then jumped inside.

Will grabbed Red by the hand and pulled her with him. They ran after them, allowing Robin to pull them up one at a time. Little John made a sharp turn toward the dirt road, and Red fell to the wooden floor as the carriage swung sideways. Robin offered her a hand, but she slapped it away then crawled to the corner and hugged her legs.

He rolled his eyes and went to sit in the opposite corner. Crossing his legs at the ankles and closing his eyes, he leaned his head back against one of the wooden crates.

Red looked at Will as he held up a papaya. After breaking it open, he handed her half. As much as she was tired of stealing, she couldn't deny her body food. She took it with a low grumble.

* * *

*A*s soon as they arrived back at Sherwood Forest, a crowd of people ran toward the carriage of food with cheerful cries. Robin jumped down and greeted Little John's nephews, allowing the kids to climb on his back. They laughed and squealed with joy, calling Robin their hero, which brought a triumphant grin to his face. Little John jumped down and distributed the food into rations to make sure everyone got an even portion according to the size of their families.

Red looked away from the hungry people. She couldn't bear to see the desperate look in their eyes. Even though she liked the feeling of bringing home food, she was tired of the life she'd been living.

She stormed away from the crowd and climbed the creaky steps to the small dwelling she shared with Robin. It consisted of two rooms above a woodshop. Even with the shutters closed, the wintery air poured inside. As she stepped in, closing the door behind her, she noted it was warmer outside.

She wasted no time in boiling a large pail of water and topping up the tin bath sitting behind a wooden divider in the corner of the room. Lying in the warm water, she closed her eyes.

Robin had no problems stealing from the rich, his justification being that they were giving back to the poor. As much as she wanted to focus on positive thoughts, Robin's words kept swirling in her mind. She needed to choose. Did she want to continue being a thief, or follow a different path?

She didn't like stealing. That much she knew. Not even from the rich. But how else were they to acquire the money needed to rebuild their village? And feed their people? She wasn't against Robin's methods entirely, but was that the life she wanted to lead for the rest of her days?

Supporting her cousin had been her life ever since her grandmother died. Taking on his responsibilities and fighting his battles was all she knew. All she'd been taught. Until Aria came along.

They would spend hours in Aria's hiding place under a tree stump, talking about what it would be like to be free. Red mostly just listened since she never considered herself to be trapped or in need of an escape. Robin never forced her to do anything she didn't want to. But she wasn't twelve anymore. Maybe it was time for a change.

She would go off on her own as soon as she caught the alpha and got her revenge.

By the time she finished her bath and got dressed, a knock came from the front door.

"Hey…" Will leaned against the open door; his damp hair smelled like eucalyptus. He'd also taken a bath. "Just thought you might be hungry." He held up a bag in his hand, and judging by the weight of it, Red could tell he'd killed something in the woods.

"Are you offering to cook?" she asked with a teasing smile, opening the door and stepping aside.

Will entered, and she closed the door behind him.

"So, did Robin send you here to check on me?" she asked, leading him toward the small kitchen in the corner of the living room. "You can tell him that I'm fine. And that I'm not running away, if that's what he's worried about."

"I'm not here because of him," Will said, drawing closer to her as he placed the bag on top of the counter. She swallowed hard at their close proximity. "I'm here because…" He leaned closer, and her cheeks turned hot. "My oven isn't working, so I need yours to cook this."

He turned away from her with a smirk, and a flutter exploded in her stomach.

"Don't worry, it's only going to take a few minutes." He started pulling ingredients out and laying them across the counter, then he selected a knife from a rack on the wall and handed it to her. "Can you peel the potatoes?"

"Sure." She took the knife and went to stand next to him.

She laid the potatoes across the wooden counter and turned them a few different ways, trying to figure out the best angle for cutting. By the time she was halfway through them, Will looked like he'd been in the kitchen for hours. Pots were steaming, garlic was sautéing, and the meat was cleaned and chopped into small, neat pieces. Will put down his knife, wiped the back of his hand across his forehead, then glanced her way with a grin.

"You're doing great."

She laughed for the first time all day. "And here I thought Little John was the only one who knew how to cook."

"My sister taught me." Will adjusted the fire, and Red sped up the rest of her chopping so she could finish and just watch him. He moved around the kitchen like he did on a job: fluid and confident, as though he was thinking ten steps ahead and knew exactly where he needed to be at all times. It was the sexiest thing she'd ever seen.

He reached for a wooden spoon then glanced her way, catching her staring. Her cheeks flamed as his creased in a smile. "Glad to see this little distraction is making you feel better," he teased. "You seemed pretty upset today."

"I…" She hesitated. "Robin was right."

"About?"

"This isn't the life I want," she said, leaning back against the counter. "Truth is, I don't want to be a thief."

She watched his reaction carefully because she wasn't sure if that was what Will wanted out of life, and she didn't want to hurt his feelings. But somehow, he always made her feel like she could tell him anything.

"Did you ever tell him that?" Will asked.

"I've tried. Several times, but he doesn't listen. It's like talking to a wall."

Will scooped up the potatoes and dumped them into a bubbling pot. It smelled amazing. She wasn't sure how it was going to be ready in a few minutes, but she wouldn't question his methods.

"I'm sorry you're not happy," he said, turning again to face her.

"It's not that," she said. "It's just…" The way he was looking at her made it hard to think. "I want *more*." The words slipped out before she could think them through, and as soon as she said them, an explosion of butterflies fluttered in her stomach. She took the knife to the basin and rinsed it so she could keep her head down.

Will leaned against the counter next to her. "You deserve more," he said, his voice low and gentle as he wiped the wooden table in front of him. "I'm sure he'll understand. And I'll back you up. If that's what you really want, of course."

A muscle in his jaw twitched, and she wondered what that meant. Did he want her to stay?

At that moment, she wanted nothing more than for him to give her a reason to. And if he did, she would grab his face and kiss every inch of it. She was suddenly beyond tired of never doing what she wanted or saying what she felt.

Will moved toward the stove and took the pan off the direct heat. "It should be ready in about ten minutes," he said, wiping his hands on a cloth.

She moved toward him until the space between them had nearly disappeared and put her hand on his arm. If nothing else, she'd wanted to do that for ages, and since she would end up leaving anyway, what was the harm in finally being bold? "So…" Her pulse started thrumming as she edged closer. "What should we do until then?"

Will's mouth curved in a slow smile. "You tell me."

She brought one hand to the back of his neck, sliding her fingers into his hair. It was softer than she expected, and his burning skin lit her up inside. She paused to catch her breath, watching the reflection of the flames dancing in his eyes. Every nerve in her body buzzed with anticipation; it was almost too much.

Will leaned in and kissed her, his lips a gentle press of heat against her mouth. It was soft and almost sweet, until she slid her arms around his neck and pulled him closer. He kissed her harder, picking her up in one smooth motion and putting her on the counter. As she instinctively wrapped her legs around his waist, the softest groan escaped him. He deepened the kiss, sending Red's heart racing. Her hands found their way to his broad shoulders, and every scattered thought she had left bouncing in her brain dissolved when his muscles contracted beneath her fingertips. They kissed until she lost all sense of time and place, and the only thing she knew was that she wanted more.

A sudden sound of approaching footsteps brought her back to herself. She pulled away and sucked in a breath, her face burning at how far up she'd pulled his shirt and the intentional way she twisted the fabric. A few seconds more, and she would have yanked it over his head.

Will seemed to have also registered the noise because he stepped back, disentangling from her. For a moment, he didn't seem to be breathing, but then he let out a long breath. She hopped off the counter, weak-kneed, and tried to smooth her hair. A second later, Robin burst in through the door.

"What are you two doing?" he asked, placing his quiver on one of the chairs. "Smells amazing."

Will cleared his throat. "Nothing much." His voice was not nearly as steady as it usually was when he talked to Robin. "I thought you were headed to the tavern?"

"I was, but then I had an idea," Robin said, walking past him and heading to the pot to smell the stew. The food wasn't ready yet, but Red was afraid that if she spoke, her voice would sound strangled and Robin would notice her flushed cheeks.

She leaned against the counter, hoping her

wobbly knees would recover sooner rather than later.

"What's wrong with you?" Robin glanced over his shoulder as he poured himself a bowl with only the vegetables and broth since the meat wasn't ready yet.

"So, what's this urgent idea that just *couldn't wait?*" she asked, not bothering to mask the irritation in her voice as she took a seat by the table. Will moved to the opposite end of the room and crossed his arms.

"So, I was thinking…" Robin took a seat across from his cousin. "There have been lots of sightings to the west—"

"It's just going to be another trap," Will cut in with an edge in his voice, and Robin cut him a confused look. It wasn't like him to respond that way, and Red couldn't help but wonder if his shift in mood had to do with what just happened between them.

Did he regret it?

"That's the problem," Robin said. "The alpha has been several steps ahead of us. He must know how Will tracks, and that's why they can throw us off their trail."

Will lowered his head, and Red hated that

he was avoiding her eyes. She should've never crossed that line. What was she thinking? Now things would be weird between them, and she hated even the thought of Will pushing her away.

"Red." Robin snapped his fingers in front of her face, ripping her back from her thoughts. "Am I talking to the wall here? Look, I'm sorry about earlier, okay? Can we please move on?"

"Fine." She leaned back in her chair and crossed her arms. "So, the alpha has been purposely throwing us off his trail. But how could the alpha possibly know our every move?"

"Who knows, they could have abilities like Aria, or…" Robin narrowed his eyes. "They could have a traitor in our camp."

Will lifted his eyes for the first time, but he didn't look at her. And as much as she tried to ignore it, it stung.

"You think someone here is sending information to the alpha?" Will asked, looking at Robin.

"I sure do, but here's the catch…" Robin's lips lifted into a cunning smile. "We find who that traitor is, then we set a trap and use him as collateral to draw out the alpha. Offer a trade."

"Shouldn't we find out who that person is first before making them collateral?" Will asked. "What if the traitor is someone we know? Maybe even someone…" His eyes shifted to her for the first time since they'd kissed. "We care about?"

Her heart soared in her chest at his subtle declaration, and when he held her gaze, she wanted nothing more than to kiss him again.

Robin slapped the table, jolting Red back to her senses. "If we have a traitor among us, I will gladly swap that coward for Marian."

"The alpha isn't going to trade Marian for just anyone," Will added, his expression a lot more serious than before. "The alpha's loyalty is to the pack, not even to one wolf alone. He won't take the bait if it means exposing the whole pack."

"How in the world do you know that?" Robin asked, giving Will a quizzical look.

"His sister," Red chimed in, and Robin looked at her. "There isn't a species in this kingdom that Belle doesn't know about."

"Belle, of course..." Robin turned to Will. "Your sister can help us!"

He arched a curious brow. "How, exactly?"

"Maybe she can help us find the *nest*."

Wolves didn't have nests, but Robin wouldn't care. He stood and paced around, his eyes wandering around the room as if the wheels in his mind were turning a million miles an hour.

"If we can catch one of them, we could use them as collateral," Robin explained. "And if the alpha doesn't respond, then we kill one wolf at a time, until we get his attention."

"You want to kill them?" Will's eyes widened in horror. "Don't you think that's a bit harsh?"

"Harsh?" Robin hissed, glaring at Will. "What are you, pro-wolf now?"

Will's gentle eyes didn't mirror Robin's scowl. "I'm just saying... we don't know enough about them to just decide to execute them. What if not all of them are bad?"

Robin took a step toward Will. "Clearly, you've never had to pick up whatever's left of your loved one after a wolf was done with them," he said acidly.

Will winced, and Red jumped to her feet. "Okay, that's enough," she said, going to stand next to him, ignoring the tightness in her chest as memories of her grandmother filled her mind. The iron scent of blood was as strong and potent as the day it covered her walls. "For the record, I am not on board with a wolf genocide either."

Robin turned to her with a huff. "Do you have any better ideas?"

"If the alpha won't trade for a wolf, then we need to figure out what it is that he *would* trade for. There's gotta be something of value he wants." Red looked at Will. "Do you think your sister would know?"

Will didn't respond. He simply kept his eyes fixed on Robin. "I don't know, but I'm due for a visit, anyway." He walked away and stormed out of the house, leaving Red aching to run after him.

She turned to Robin. "What is wrong with you?"

He waved it off as he collapsed on the chair and returned to his meal. "He'll be fine."

"You can't just treat people like that then

sweep it under the rug, Robin." She stepped in his line of sight, forcing him to look up at her. "And is your obsession with Marian that strong that we don't even matter to you anymore?"

He stared at her for a long time. "*I'm* obsessed? What about your plan to capture the alpha all by yourself? Did you even stop to think what losing you would do to me?"

His confession, though hurtful, was sincere, and it caught Red off guard. She was the only family he had left, but she didn't always think that mattered to him.

He looked down at his steaming bowl, dipped the bread in the stew, and took a large bite. Just like that, he was done talking.

She touched his shoulder, but he didn't respond. There was so much she wanted to say to him, but only a soft sigh escaped her lips. Their relationship was complicated, but it didn't mean she didn't care about him. And now she knew that he cared about her just the same. But they would be okay, and she gave his shoulder a light squeeze as an assurance.

Red grabbed her cloak and stepped outside just as Will galloped away on his horse.

She called out to him, but he didn't turn around. She jumped onto Scout, and after throwing the hood over her head to make both of them invisible, she followed Will into the night.

CHAPTER 6

*A*fter some time, Will's horse grew weary and slowed to a canter. The bright moonlight lit up the path ahead and cast ugly shadows of monster-like trees with claws for hands on either side of him. But Will paid his surroundings no attention as he ran his tongue over his lips, replaying the kiss he shared with Red.

He could still taste her, and her sweet scent was all over his clothes. It warmed his heart as he rode through the cold night. No one else crossed his path. The villagers had grown fearful of wolves, and they'd never venture out into the woods after dark. Least of all during a full moon.

His eyes looked up at the glowing orb in the darkened sky. A soft halo of light surrounded it, and its silvery rays were like beads of energy, soaring through his veins. Bathing in the moonlight gave him more focus and better clarity. And tonight he needed it.

Red had claimed him with her pretty rosebud lips and gripped onto him with such force, it made him smile. Despite being petite and barely up to his shoulders, she was fierce.

But then Robin's words cut through his vision like a bloody knife.

"Clearly, you've never had to pick up whatever's left of your loved one after a wolf was done with them."

Will looked down at the saddle and gripped the leather reins with all of his might. As if sensing his tension, the horse stopped and snorted.

"Easy, Pedigree, it's okay." He shushed the horse, smoothing her mane with his fingertips as he forced his legs to relax. Pedigree was the only one who would tolerate him enough to let him ride. The other horses were wary of him. Probably aware that he wasn't fully human. And they were right to fear him.

Wolves were dangerous. They hunt. They kill.

As much as he wanted to forget, the truth would always remain the same. A wolf had killed Red's grandmother, and for that reason alone, he could never be with her. Will's stomach tied into knots. If she discovered who he was—*what* he really was—she would never accept him. He could already picture the horror in her eyes if she ever found out the truth. She would run away and never look at him, ever again.

Just the thought of causing Red that degree of pain crushed his heart.

He needed to cool off. Lying to Red about his true identity was unfair to her and would only lead to heartache. He inhaled her scent on his shirt and frowned. It was stronger, somehow.

A twig snapped at a distance behind him, and his ears pricked up. His nostrils flared as he inhaled the strong, sweet scent of Red. She couldn't be more than half a mile away. He grinned to himself, knowing she must have thought he had no idea she was tracking him.

Will pushed on until he reached a river. He

jumped down and filled his sheepskin flask as Pedigree gratefully stopped to drink.

Will wasn't sure what time it was. Under the moon, he was never tired. If anything, he was more alert and awake now than he'd ever been during the day. But he picked up Red's ragged breaths even though she was still far away.

The journey to Belle's place would take another day at least, and Will knew that Red was just as stubborn as her cousin. If not more. She'd follow him until her horse collapsed and then continue on foot if that was what it would take.

He considered blowing her cover, but then he'd have to face her. And seeing that he was not even a bit tired, lying down next to her at a campfire sounded like asking for trouble. He tied up his horse and removed the saddle to let her breathe.

He laid on the ground and rested his hands under his head as he looked up at the starry sky. When the sound of horses' hooves grew loud, he was certain Red had caught up. Will peeked through squinted eyes to see her. But there was still nothing. Only rustling leaves on the path. Maybe she wasn't ready to face it all just yet. Maybe she was still collecting her thoughts. He wasn't entirely sure what he would say either if she appeared to him at the moment, but one thing was certain, her taste was still on his lips.

He closed his eyes and focused on the faint sound of her racing heartbeat. She was nervous. At least he wasn't the only one.

Will turned over, allowing his breath to slow as the clouds covered the moon. Then, as if caught under a spell, a wave of sleepiness washed over him, and he found himself unable to stop the sickly charming dreams involving Red and her juicy lips.

* * *

The next day, Will kept a safe distance from Red. Only when he saw the little log cabin with a smoking chimney on the crest of a hill did he stop and turn back. It took almost an hour for her to catch up.

"You can show yourself now, we're almost at Belle's," he called back. A small gasp followed, then Red finally appeared, as did Scout.

Within a few seconds, her horse was next to his. "How did you know?" she asked, giving him the biggest scowl he'd ever seen her muster. The sight of her dark brows knitted made him smirk.

"I'm a tracker, remember?"

Red shot him a suspicious look. "You can track people... behind you?"

Will shook his head with a laugh as he encouraged his horse to continue. He couldn't think of a convincing lie to tell, so he opted to not reply at all. Red joined him, her horse cantering beside his.

"It's a good thing we're here. I am starving," Red said, dismounting. Will nipped his bottom lip with guilt. He had been so lost inside his head, he barely stopped to give his horse a break, let alone hunt. Their stew back at the village seemed like a week ago. His stomach grumbled.

"Don't worry, Belle will have something for us." Will jumped down as they walked past the manor's gate. Belle was a caretaker of the mansion, which belonged to King of the

Shores. But she had her own small log cabin in the far end of the property. Once they were close enough, a flickering light appeared in one of the windows, and the door flew open.

"Will!" Belle greeted him cheerfully. "I thought I heard you coming!"

A flash of dark hair obscured Will's vision as Belle flung herself into his arms. She squeezed him so tightly, it almost took his breath away. He chuckled as they broke apart, and she rested her hands on his cheeks, grinning at him.

"You look older. It's been too long," she said.

Will smirked and resisted the urge to roll his eyes. "It hasn't been *that* long."

But Belle wasn't looking at him anymore. Her eyes widened as she looked past him. "Red! I'm so happy to see you!"

Will turned and watched Belle and Red hug. Belle cradled Red's face and kissed her on each cheek, prompting Red to squirm away. "Okay, okay, enough kissing already." They laughed, then Belle threw her arm around Red's shoulder and they started to walk to the cabin.

"Come on, I've got rabbit stew bubbling on the stove," Belle said. But Will couldn't take his eyes off of Red. Her cheeks flushed as she beamed at him, warming his heart. Visions crossed his mind of a make-believe world where Red and Belle would be sisters-in-law, and they could play happy families. But then the clouds parted, and the silver moonlight sent a rush of adrenaline through his whole body. He curled his fingers and balled his hands into fists.

Sure, they'd play happy families until Red found out *what* he was. He shook away the dark thought with a frown. "I'll be right in, just gotta take care of the horses," he said, sounding far too breezy to not raise suspicion. But if he had raised the alarm, neither Belle nor Red gave it away.

"I'll see you inside," Belle said as she led Red into the cabin. Will waved at her, but as the door shut behind her, his smile faded.

He tended to the horses deep in thought. As always, a single memory played on repeat. Like it had, for the past six years. Still fresh in his mind, as if time could never erase it.

Will gritted his teeth. If he had done as he

was told... his brother would still be alive. And he would've never been banished from the pack.

His thoughts then moved to Red. He remembered her face, illuminated in the candlelight as she looked out of the little window of her grandmother's house. The full moon shone brilliantly, and a howl of agony filled the air, casting a heavy cloud of depression over the area. He was in wolf form, and there was no way Red would know it was him. But none of that mattered at the time. The deep metallic scent of blood was so strong, he picked it up miles away. If he hadn't been so far from Red... would he have been able to save her grandmother?

So many horrors. So many regrets. Which only cemented his decision that he would never be good enough for Red. She deserved someone who was kind and good—like her. Someone human.

He locked up the stables and returned to the cabin with his jaw clenched and a pang in his heart. As he walked through the door, the overwhelming scent of spices and burning oils made him wrinkle his nose, and he turned to

find Red curled up by the fire wrapped in a
blanket. Her hair lay damp over her shoulders,
and the heat of the flames made her cheeks
rosy.

"What took you so long?" she asked,
looking up as he shut the door. Belle entered
the room with a bundle of blankets and thrust
them into Will's chest.

"Your turn to wash. I've just topped up the
bath with hot water," she said, pinching her
nose closed. Will glanced at Red, who stifled a
laugh.

"Go on, you'll feel loads better, and there's
a bowl of stew with your name on it."

The tin bath sat outside, behind the cabin.
There was little privacy as Will undressed and
slipped into the water. But he didn't worry
about travelers that might pass by. He bit his
tongue, hardly daring to breathe as he listened
to Red and Belle's conversation. He knew they
would have thought it impossible for him to
listen in, and he wouldn't usually eavesdrop,
but Red and Belle were talking about *him*.

"Will may be too proud to admit it, but..."
Red's voice was soft. "I could tell he misses
you. He always talks about your cooking and

all these little things you taught him growing up. And even though you're only three years older, he talks about you like you're his mother."

Will didn't have to see his sister to know she was smiling.

"I miss having him around too, but I think it's been good for him to join Robin," Belle confessed. "He needed a strong leadership figure to fill the void left by his brother, and that's just not something I was able to do."

"Wait, Will has a brother?"

"Had," Belle corrected, sadness evident in her tone. "He died in combat when Will was just fifteen years old."

The shock in Red's voice was unmistakable. "I had no idea. I mean, he never said anything."

"I'm not surprised," Belle said. "It may have been years ago, but it still hurts like it was yesterday, and Will is not one to talk about sad things."

"No, he certainly isn't. Were you all close?"

Belle hummed. "His brother was my best friend. I still remember the day we met. I was coming home from the field and I found him half-dead on the road. He had fallen into a wolf trap set up by one of the hunters in the forest."

Will tensed at the mention of the wolf trap, but Belle corrected herself.

"And you know, when a human gets caught in one of those, they're lucky to survive at all. So, I brought him home and tended to his wounds until he was better. Soon after that, I met Will and they both became like brothers to me."

"If you cared for Will, why send him off with Robin?" Red asked.

"I only sent him off to Robin after his brother died," Belle explained. "But only because a man needs to learn leadership. And Robin was the safest option at the time."

"Yeah, well, lately he's been a hazard to us all."

Belle chuckled. "He may be rough around the edges, but he cares deeply, and that's what makes him a good leader. Reckless at times, yes. But a good leader, nonetheless."

"So, I take it you've heard about his quest to save Marian?" Red asked.

"Word gets around."

"It's not that I don't want to save her," Red explained. "At first, I wanted him to save Marian, but this has become an all-consuming conquest. He's fixated on the idea of Marian from the pages The Intruder gave him... but what if she isn't that person anymore?"

"Regardless of who she is, the potential to be the person from those pages will always exist," Belle explained. "And that's probably what he's holding on to."

"Do you think I have a story?" Red asked.

"I think we all have a story," Belle said. "But you should be glad that you don't know yours because it can really mess with your head. Look at Robin...he's living proof of that."

"Did The Intruder mess with your head, too?"

"Oh, The Intruder did a number on me. But that is a story for another day." Belle laughed, and only someone who knew her as well as Will did could hear the pain in it. "Anyway, as good as it is to see you both, why don't you cut to the chase and tell me why you're really here?"

"Right." Red paused as if trying to put it into words. "Well, long story short, we have failed miserably at every attempt to track the alpha."

"The alpha wolf?" Belle asked, surprised. "Red, you can't track a wolf. They have hyper-sensitive senses. Not only could they smell your scent from miles away, they hear you breathe from just as far."

"Wow, I had no idea. But that actually makes a lot of sense," Red admitted. "Anyway, that's why we're here. We need to change strategy. We need to make the alpha come to us."

"How do you intend to do that?" Belle asked.

"We need to find something more valuable to the alpha than Marian," Red explained. "Then at least we can—"

"Arrange a trade," Belle finished Red's thought.

"Exactly."

"That's actually pretty genius," Belle admitted. "What does Will think of this plan?"

"Well, it was either this or a wolf geno-cide," Red joked without the need to add that it was Robin's idea. "Which, to be honest, I didn't think he would be on board with that at all."

"Why not?"

"Will is too kind. He would never go for something so vicious."

"But *you* would?"

Red neither confirmed nor denied. "Personally, I'm only interested in killing one wolf."

"The one who killed your grandmother?"

Red was silent for a long time, and Will wished he could hear her thoughts.

"I saw him once, you know," she finally said, her voice soft. "The day my Grams died, I heard him howl outside, and when I went to the window, I saw him in the forest. He had light brown fur and amber eyes. It's been six years, but I will never forget that monster."

"Saving Marian and wanting to kill the alpha are two entirely different battles, Red," Belle warned. "I just don't want you to do anything you'd regret."

"And why would I regret killing a wolf?" Red asked, disgusted. "They're wild savages."

Red's words pierced Will's heart like a

dagger. Her hatred for wolves ran a lot deeper than she let on, and it burned like acid through his veins.

"So… can you help us?" Red asked.

"How could I be of assistance?"

"Do you have any idea what would be valuable to a wolf?"

"Other than a bone?" Belle joked in her dry humor, but Red didn't laugh. "Look, I have no idea, but… if there is such information out there… there's only one place you would find it."

Will leaned in, hanging onto every word coming out of Belle's mouth.

"Where?" Red asked.

Belle sucked in a deep breath. "The trolls."

* * *

*I*n the middle of the night, Will stared up at the living room ceiling, unable to sleep. As hard as he tried, he couldn't get Red out of his mind. The taste of her lips was branded on his brain, beckoning for more. And knowing she was sleeping in his old room, in his bed, and his sheets would smell like her, did things to his mind and heart that he hadn't been used to.

A noise in the kitchen snapped him from his thoughts, and he sat up. The faint light of a candle burned in the corner, and Will pulled off his covers to check who was awake in the middle of the night.

He should've known it was Red. Her scent would've given her away had the smell of Belle's herbs not been so strong and overwhelming in the house.

"Oh, sorry. Did I wake you?" she asked, grabbing a cloth and removing a pot of boiling water from the fire. "I couldn't sleep, so I thought to have some tea. Do you want some?"

"I'm okay."

"Where are the mugs?" she asked, looking around.

"On the top by that cabinet." Will pointed to it, but soon realized Red would probably have to hop on the counter like a frog, and as clumsy as she could be, she would end up breaking something and waking Belle. "Here, I'll get it." He squeezed by her just as she turned around. When her cheeks flushed, he thought maybe it would've been a good idea to have put on a shirt. He pushed past her in the small space, and she looked away. After grabbing the mug, he placed it on the table and stepped back to watch her pour a handful of leaves inside it before filling it with hot water.

She picked up the mug and held it securely in her hands, warming her fingers. When she took a careful sip, his eyes locked on her rosy lips, and the urge to kiss her hit him like a brick wall.

He sucked in a breath and looked away. "Well, good night."

"Things don't have to be weird with us, you know," she said over her steaming cup, and Will turned to look at her. "What happened back at my place clearly didn't mean anything. We were tired and hungry, and not thinking straight."

There was a twinkle in her eyes that didn't quite match her words, but he didn't question it. Getting things back to normal was probably for the best.

"I mean, two friends can kiss and it doesn't

mean anything." She didn't sound so sure, but he could tell she wanted to believe that. "Besides, just because you kiss someone, doesn't mean you have to have feelings for them, right?"

When their eyes met, Will could hear her heartbeat racing. "Right," he agreed as he moved slowly toward her, his eyes glued to hers. "No feelings at all."

"Exactly," she muttered, her voice wavering as he drew closer. "We'll always be just friends."

He stopped in front of her, his face inches from hers. "Friends... who kiss."

"Only on occasion," she whispered, almost breathless.

Will put a tentative arm around her. "And it doesn't mean anything."

She sighed and leaned into him. "Nothing at all."

A strand of hair tumbled across her eye and he pushed it back, and before he knew it, both of his hands were cupping her cheeks. Red's eyes were steady on his, her lips curved in a small, questioning smile. He drew her face closer, and before he could come to his senses, he kissed her.

Her mouth was soft and warm, and it tasted like mint. She put the mug down behind her and heat spread through him slowly as she slid her warm hands up his chest and around the back of his neck. Then she nipped lightly at his bottom lip, and the heat turned into an electric jolt. He wrapped his arms around her and lifted her up. Her legs wrapped around his waist as he took her to the couch. He pulled her onto his lap, kissing her lips and the skin between her jaw and her collarbone. She pushed him back against the pillows and molded her body to his, and Will's entire body buzzed with excitement.

A loud, clattering noise made them freeze. Somehow they had dislodged the candle holder and sent it flying across the floor.

"Will?" Red sat up at the sound of Belle's voice, which was much too close for someone who was supposed to be in her room. "Is everything all right?"

"Fine," he said as they disentangled. "I just knocked down your candle thing. Sorry about that."

They put a foot between them on the couch, both of them red-faced and flushed, waiting for Belle's response.

"Oh, okay. I'm getting some tea. Do you want some?"

"No thanks." He'd already tasted enough tea on Red's tongue, which just about sent his mind reeling again. Red tried to get her curls under control while his hands itched to mess them up again.

"What about you, Red?" Belle asked.

"I'm good, thanks." Red jumped to her feet and rushed back to the room. Belle appeared by the hall and gave Will a parental look. But her concern wasn't about him being with a girl. It was with him being with a *human* girl. And none other than someone who hated wolves, at that.

She didn't have to say anything. He knew it was a mistake. "Good night," he said, turning his back to her and closing his eyes. Though he knew sleep would be the farthest thing from his mind.

* * *

*T*he next morning, Will woke up to the scent of Belle's cooking. Red sat at the little wooden table, wrapped in a blanket and her hair frizzing at the ends. She looked up as he entered the room, and her smile lit a fire in his soul. He had never felt better and worse at the same time. The guilt for kissing her a second time eroded all feelings of joy that might've risen from knowing she kissed him back.

"Belle's gone out to get more firewood. She's made us breakfast, and I don't want to ever leave," Red said before taking greedy gulps of water.

Will smiled as he pulled on his boots. "You don't want to leave because someone made you eggs?"

Red nodded giddily. "Not just normal eggs. She's seasoned them. My mouth won't stop watering."

Will sat and devoured his food, shoveling them into his mouth without barely taking a breath. Red's dark brows shot up as she watched him. "Did you even taste that?"

Will downed his milk and flashed her a

proud smile. "I'm going to tend to the horses," he said, rising to his feet.

"Oh, sure, leave me to clean up all this by myself," Red teased, pointing to the dirty dishes.

Will gave a light shrug. "I would love to stay and help, but..." Her natural scent was strong and delicious in every way. Just thinking about it made him weak at the knees. "I need some fresh air."

Red shot him a suspicious look. "Are you okay?"

"The spices that my sister uses." He pointed around the house. "They're a bit too strong for me."

Red's eyes narrowed. "You're lying. Okay, fine. Go. But don't give Scout any apples. She's allergic, remember?"

Will rolled his eyes playfully as he made for the door. "Only you would have a horse allergic to apples. Besides, we haven't seen any for weeks."

Red didn't argue. With the harsh winter weather, it made the woods appear barren.

As he entered the stables, he caught Belle brushing Pedigree's mane, her face troubled.

But she looked up as he approached, and her frown turned into a rehearsed smile.

"Penny for your thoughts?" Will asked. Belle's cheeks dimpled as her smile took a more natural shape at the inside joke. It was a phrase found in one of Belle's favorite books. Neither of them knew what a penny was exactly, but she had always asked him that whenever Will seemed lost in thought.

Fond memories flashed across his mind's eye of a younger Belle sitting with a young Will on the floor, rubbing his back or dabbing his tears with a cloth. She was not a blood relative, but ever since his brother died, she was the only family he had left.

"Red got me thinking about your brother last night," Belle said as she continued brushing Pedigree. "If I miss him this much, I can't even imagine how you must feel."

Will picked up a brush and joined Belle. "Some days are better than others."

"How come you never told her about him?"

Will stopped brushing and thought about it. "Red is a smart girl. Too smart for her own good, actually." A smile lifted the corner of his lips as her image flashed in his mind. "And since most of my memories with my brother consists of him training me on how to be a wolf, I was afraid that I would slip up, and she would put the pieces together and find out what I am."

Belle put the brush down and turned to him. "*Who* you truly are is Will Scarlet. The most loving and loyal person I have ever known, and no amount of fur is ever going to change that."

She ruffled his hair, and he chuckled. "Well, you have to say that because you love me."

"True…" Belle cocked her head to the side with a lopsided grin. "But what makes you think she doesn't?"

"She doesn't know *what* I am, Belle."

"Then tell her."

Will let out a laugh. "Okay, clearly, you've been inhaling too many spices."

Belle remained serious. "She deserves to know, Will."

"I know." He let out a long breath then plopped down on a block of hay. "It's just that I know the moment she finds out, it's going to crush her. And just the thought of causing her any degree of pain is unbearable."

"You're in love with her, aren't you?" Belle's question was like a bolt of lightning across his chest. He winced as he pressed his eyes shut. "All the more reason you shouldn't keep leading her on without telling her the truth."

"Don't you think I know that?" He stood and turned away from his sister, gazing toward the snow-covered mountains in the distance. "But she's my weakness, Belle. She's the only one who has the potential to destroy me from inside out."

"That's the good thing about wolves," Belle reminded him. "They're not easily defeated. When they're thrown down, they always get up with their head held high."

"This is different." Will frowned. "I have replayed in my mind every possible scenario, and there hasn't been a single one where she forgives me."

Belle came to stand next to him and rested her hand on his shoulder. "That's because that unforgiving voice inside your head is your own, not hers. Maybe if you give her the chance, she'll surprise you."

"Or…" He looked at his sister again. "We could find that cure you were looking into. You know, get rid of the wolf once and for all."

Belle narrowed her eyes. "Didn't you give me strict orders to stop looking for that cure?"

"Did you listen?"

"Of course not, but that's only because I never listen to you." She smiled as she picked up the brush again and moved toward Scout. "But is that what you really want?"

Will shrugged away and paced the barn, conflicted. If he wasn't a wolf, then he could live a normal life, maybe even be with Red. The thought was heartening, but if he wasn't a wolf, he'd lose his very identity. Besides, being a wolf was the only connection to his brother he had left, and giving that up would be like giving up on everything his brother wanted for him.

"I don't know." He went back to brushing Pedigree, trying hard to ignore the tug-of-war inside his mind. "Just keep me updated on what you find."

"You know… your brother always said you would make a great alpha one day."

"Alpha?" Will laughed as he picked up a bucket of old root vegetables and emptied it in a trough. "Yeah, like that will ever happen."

"Why do you think he was training you so hard?" Belle asked.

"I always thought he liked torturing me," Will joked.

"Well, that he did, but there was a reason for his madness. And if you ask me, I still think you can."

"Can what?"

"Challenge the alpha. Give him the boot. Take his place."

"Okay…" Will dropped the bucket and turned to his sister. He lowered his voice as his eyes flickered to the doors, worried that Red might walk in. "You may think you know a lot about wolves, but here's a little detail to add to your collection… *banished* wolves can't challenge an alpha, unless the alpha challenges them first. Besides, I wouldn't know the first thing about being a leader."

"I wouldn't be so sure." She flashed him a

confident smile. "But anyway, I guess we're back to square one then."

Will arched a brow. "Which is?"

Belle stopped brushing Scout and cleared her throat. Her gaze darted to the barn doors before returning to Will. "To find a cure," she said in a low voice.

"Ah, that." Will picked up another bucket of old vegetables and emptied it in a trough.

"I don't think that's the answer for you, either, but..." She placed a hand on his shoulder and squeezed. He took in the motherly look in her eyes. "I just want you to be happy."

The barn door swung open with a creak and Red appeared. "Hey, what are we talking about?" she asked, boldly walking toward them, her arms swinging. Will exchanged looks with Belle.

"Belle was just telling me a bit more about the trolls," he said, motioning for Belle to talk.

She shot him a look before clearing her throat.

"Do tell," Red said anxiously, her expression hopeful.

Belle sighed. "They are sweet and pose no

threat, but... they do speak in riddles, so if you want any information from them, you will have to play along with their mind-bending games."

"What if we get it wrong?" Red asked.

Belle put a hand on Will's shoulder, all the while keeping her eyes on Red. "Then honesty will get you what you need."

Before Will could ask what she meant, Belle threw the brush aside and wiped her hand on her sheepskin jacket. "Well, it's always a pleasure to have you both come and visit, but if you don't want to get stuck in a blizzard, you should head out soon." She gave Will's shoulder another light squeeze before heading out of the barn. "I'll pack some food for you to take."

Will looked up at the gray sky and watched as thick clouds rolled in.

"I didn't know there was a storm coming," Red said, and Will turned to look at her. Her cheeks were rosy from the cold wind.

There was definitely a storm brewing, he wanted to say, but if only she knew it had nothing to do with the weather.

CHAPTER 7

$\mathcal{R}$ed tightened her cloak around her petite frame as her teeth chattered against the bitter blizzard.

"I don't think we can keep going like this!" Will yelled above the howling wind while riding on his horse next to Red. She nodded, her face numb.

"I see a cave up ahead," Will said. "Let's see if we can break camp there. At least until the blizzard passes."

He galloped ahead and jumped off his horse. Red followed and dismounted her horse so he could shield her from the piercing wind. Will came back within a few seconds, and they guided their horses into the mouth of the cave, just enough to be shielded from the winds.

"Aria has really outdone herself this time," Will said, shaking the wetness out of his hair.

"This isn't Aria, remember?" Red said, removing the saddle from Scout's back. "It's Jack. I hope he made it to the Ice Mountains to find out how to control his powers. I don't know how much more of this I can take."

"Doesn't seem like he's figured it out yet," Will mumbled as he unsaddled his horse.

"Looks like someone's already been here," Red said, pointing to a pile of ash in the corner.

"Do you think there's enough there to make a new fire?" Will asked.

Red went to check. She crouched over the ashy wood and poked at it. "I think so, but it might not burn for long." She turned to look at Will and spotted him changing his cotton shirt. A wave of heat washed over her, and she shifted her attention back to the pile of ash on the floor. The sudden image of them kissing the night before flashed in her mind.

They still hadn't talked about that kiss. And what a kiss. If it hadn't been so good, it would've been much easier to ignore, but it was earth-shattering. She'd kissed other boys before, but nothing had ever felt like *that*. No one had ever made her want *more*.

She shook her head, hoping those thoughts would crumble like a pile of snow, but they were etched in her brain like ice. Grabbing a couple of rocks, she began to strike them against each other until sparks appeared. By the time she got the fire going, Will had finished tending to the horses and came to sit in front of the fire, across from her. She would've preferred he sat next to her, but after what happened the night before, maybe the distance was for the best.

She looked up to see the reflection of the fire dancing in his hazel eyes. He wasn't looking at her though, and for a moment she wondered if he was avoiding her. Was their friendship going to suffer because of their stupid lack of self-control?

He stretched out his hand to the fire, warming his fingers, and she looked away before he caught her staring. Grabbing a stick, she poked the log a few times.

"Belle told me about your brother," Red

said, her voice soft above the crackling of the flames. "I'm very sorry for your loss."

Will shrugged, keeping his eyes on the fire. "It was a long time ago."

"Yeah, but I'm sure it still hurts," Red said. "She said he died in combat. What happened?"

Will watched the fire dance between them for a long time, seeming unsure whether or not he wanted to talk about it.

"I'm sorry. I shouldn't have asked."

"It's okay." He looked up for the first time and met her eyes. "The truth is, I don't really know what happened that night because he told me to leave. And now I just keep looping in my head the idea that if I hadn't left... maybe he would still be alive." He shifted his gaze back to the fire, and Red frowned.

"I used to think the same way," she said, following his gaze toward the flames. "For years, I blamed myself for leaving my Grams alone. That maybe if I hadn't gone apple picking that day, then I could've gotten her to safety somehow."

"That's not fair. You were only twelve."

"And you were only fifteen." She waited

for him to meet her eyes again. "The point is, we don't know how things would've turned out had we made a different decision, but what we do know is... we can't change the past. And it isn't fair for us to carry that guilt for the rest of our lives. I know my Grams wouldn't want that for me. Would your brother want that for you?"

Will shook his head. "Of course not."

"Then I think it's time for us to shift the blame to where it belongs," she said, narrowing her eyes. "To those who killed them."

"There's still the guilt of moving on without them, though."

Red nodded. "Yes, there is, but at least for me, seeking revenge for her death gives me something to hold on to," she said, reaching for her bag and pulling out the jar.

"What's that?" Will asked.

She held up the jar. "It's an adronna plant."

"What's it for?"

Red poured out some of the leaves from inside the jar then pulled out a pair of gloves.

"Are those Aria's gloves?" he asked, narrowing his eyes.

"Yes, they are." Red slipped them on then posed. "Don't they look fancy? I feel so royal."

Will chuckled while Red shifted her attention back to the plant. She picked up a leaf then held it over the fire just enough to let it catch. Once the leaf shriveled like a wick, she dropped it into the jar with the others and watched as it lit up in front of her. She pulled away from the flame and used a stick from the ground to swirl the mixture.

Before long, the fire burned out, and all that was left was a tiny puddle of tar. She grabbed one of her arrows from her quiver and dipped the tip into the mixture.

Will's curious eyes stayed on her the whole time.

She jumped to her feet and looked down at Will with a smile. "Come and see."

Will stood and followed her to the mouth of the cave. She looked at the trees and narrowed her eyes, trying to see past the blizzard. She caught sight of a squirrel on a branch and nocked the arrow in her bow. She took aim and released the arrow into the woods. A faint thud echoed in the distance, and she turned to Will with a smile.

"I think it worked!"

He gave her a quizzical look. "It's not like you never killed a squirrel before."

"I didn't kill him." She grabbed Will's arm and pulled him with her. After a few minutes of rummaging through the bushes, Will found the animal and they ran back to the cave.

Will opened his hand to find a terrified squirrel looking up at him. Red scooped him up and examined the small cut on his leg where her arrow had grazed him.

"Is he frozen?" Will asked, looking over her shoulder.

"He's paralyzed," she explained, rolling him over on her palm. "Sorry, little fella. I'll tell you what…" She rubbed his belly. "I'll keep you safe until you can move again. How's that?"

"How long will that take?" Will asked.

She turned to answer him. Surprised at how close he was, she gasped. The scent of soap still lingered on his skin, and she had to fight the urge to lean into him. If they kissed again, there was no one to interrupt them here. They would definitely cross the line.

She cleared her throat, and Will stepped back.

"Probably a couple of hours," she said, shifting her attention to the squirrel again. "But that's all I need to catch that wolf."

Will lowered his eyes with a frown, and she nudged him with her shoulder. "You don't have to worry about me." She gave him a reassuring smile. "With the adronna plant, I'll paralyze the alpha and he won't even be able to touch me."

She walked further into the cave and sat back in front of the fire, still holding the animal in her hands.

"Can I ask you a question?" He leaned back on the rock wall and crossed his legs at the ankles. "How do you know it was the alpha who killed your grandmother?"

Memories of that day invaded Red's mind like a tsunami, and her eyes dropped to the fire that was still burning between them. "The Intruder told me," she said, her voice soft above the crackling of the flames. "And I know what he looks like because I saw him.

That day, when I found my grandmother on the floor, he was outside. In the woods. His fur was light brown and his eyes a golden yellow." She looked up to meet Will's horrified stare, the reflection of the dancing flames illuminated his hazel eyes. "When I see him again... I'll know."

* * *

*R*ed took Will's hand and allowed him to pull her up to the top of Troll's Peak. Sweat dripped down their faces, and she bent over to lean on her knees, breathless.

The climb to the top was so harsh, they had to leave their horses halfway up the mountain. At least the blizzard had cleared. As they looked over the crest of the mountain top, Red stopped in her tracks, taken aback by the view.

The rocky, red terrain below made it like they had walked into a different continent. Evergreen trees stood like broccoli florets, and all manner of flowers blossomed in the cracks between the rocks. A wide river opened out to a lake, and the rushing sound of water echoed in the air.

Belle's directions were copied from an old map. Had Red not trusted Belle with her life, she would have listened to her own reservations. Many people in the Chanted Forest had not even heard of trolls. If Red were to tell the people in the tavern that Troll's Peak was a pocket of heaven with flourishing foliage, trees with every shade of green leaves and crystal clear water, she'd be laughed at.

The way to the mountain top continued in the form of a narrow path.

In her peripheral vision, Red noticed Will's hands hovering at either side, as if ready to catch her if she lost her balance. She smirked. Ever since she could walk, she climbed trees and wasn't afraid of heights.

They walked until the path ended and fell away over the edge of a cliff. Red moved closer to the edge with Will beside her, then looked down at the ravine dividing the two mountains and wondered how they would get across.

Just then, a rock the size of a horse's head rolled down the other side of the mountain, stopping at the edge of the cliff across from them. The ground beneath their feet trembled and Will grasped Red's waist as they struggled to keep their balance. The large rock changed form, revealing a small woman with blue peonies atop her head. Her gray skin had cracks around the eyes and mouth, with a pair of pink eyes which sparkled like a pair of kunzite gemstones.

Red grabbed onto Will's arm with an excited squeal. Belle was right—trolls were real, and they were more enchanting than Red could have ever imagined.

"Welcome," the troll greeted them from the other side with a warm smile. Though she was the size of a child, the troll's voice was rich and warm, and it echoed through the mountain as she stared at them with curious eyes. "My name is Neptune. I sense you're in need of help?"

"We're seeking information," Will answered.

"Regarding?"

"The wolves," Red chimed in.

"I see." Neptune brought a finger to her thin lips and looked down in thought. "If you're seeking the identity of the wolves, we are not at liberty to share."

Will let out a sigh which sounded like a mixture of relief and tension. He had been acting a bit weird since they arrived, but there was no time to worry about him right now. Red shook her head and turned to the troll.

"What *can* you tell us about them?" she asked.

Neptune smiled and opened her arms as if inviting Red into a hug. But there was a gap between them that couldn't be crossed without a bridge. "Only the pure of heart are worthy of answers. It is the only way to ensure that the information given will not be used for evil."

Red and Will traded glances briefly.

"What must we do to prove ourselves?" Will asked.

"You must reveal to me your darkest secret," Neptune said, backing away from the edge. "If the stones find you worthy, you will know."

That was a tall order. Red looked at Will again. All color had drained from his face, and he tugged at the collar of his brown raiment as if it were suffocating him.

She frowned momentarily, then turned back to the troll. "I can go first," she said, puffing out her chest, bracing herself. "Our village didn't burn because of Aria. The Evil Queen did it because of *me*."

She could feel Will's eyes on her, but she didn't look at him.

"The Evil Queen knew that Aria was staying with us," Red confessed. "So she made a deal with me. If I gave up Aria, she would capture the alpha and hand him over. I was so desperate and driven by hatred that I agreed."

Will stared at Red in shock. But she forced herself to ignore it as she continued.

"But I couldn't go through with it. I told Aria what I had done, and that's why she left. When The Queen found out I protected Aria, she burned our village."

There was a long moment of silence, and Red wondered if her confession wasn't pure enough to appease the rocks. But then the ground trembled, and Will pulled her away from the edge of the cliff.

Thousands of rocks rolled toward the edge

like a magnet to metal and merged, beginning to form a rocky plank over the opening between Red and the troll.

But the rocks stopped forming, leaving an incomplete plank hanging in the air.

Neptune looked at Will, indicating it was his turn, and he sucked in a nervous breath. Red didn't want to intrude in his deepest secret, but she couldn't help but be intrigued. Will was always so transparent. What dark secret could he possibly have?

Will steeled himself, keeping his eyes on the troll. "I knew Red was there when I was bathing at the waterfall that one time."

The troll simply smiled, and Will grunted, knowing he needed to reveal more.

"And... kissing her meant more to me than I let on."

Red's heart soared in her chest, but why did he keep that a secret?

The ground trembled again, but this time Will didn't hold on to Red. Was he embarrassed about his confession? There was no time to dwell on that, though. More rocks gravitated to one another until the rocky plank formed a complete bridge.

The troll lifted her arms and invited them to cross over to the other mountain where she stood. Will took the lead, stepping carefully onto the bridge. It seemed firm and steady, and Red followed close behind.

As they reached the other side, Neptune turned on her heels and led them down a winding path, disappearing through a wall of vines. Once through, Red held her breath, almost choking on the fragrant flowers surrounding them. Thousands of trolls sat on raised stone seating, shaped like an amphitheater. A sea of eyes watched them walk to the center where a huge well stood. Green vines climbed the wall of the well, and pink and yellow peonies grew out of the cracks in the stone.

Neptune stopped beside the well and nodded to a short male troll, who struggled with the wooden handle. Red considered offering her help but thought it might cause offense. A few minutes passed, and the troll pushed a small wooden bucket full of glittering water toward Red.

"Please. Drink," Neptune said as the male

troll passed Red a ladle. All eyes were on them as she took it.

"What is this for?" Red asked.

"This is the Fount of Knowledge. If you want information, you must drink."

Will looked at the troll shrewdly and sniffed. An odd reaction, but Red wasn't surprised. Trolls had a distinct earthy smell. Like smoldering wood on a bonfire.

Will nodded to Red. "It's a symbol of trust," he whispered. "If we show that we trust them enough to drink this, they will trust us with what they know."

Though still hesitant, she trusted Will. As she drank the water, the liquid rolled down her throat like honey. It soothed her soul and cleared her mind.

"Now..." Neptune beamed, taking a seat in front of them. "How can I be of assistance?"

"The alpha took something from us," Will said, crouching to her level. "But in order to get it back, we need to find something valuable enough to offer as a trade. What would be valuable enough to the alpha?"

The troll hummed for a moment. "Something of value to the alpha… enough for them to relinquish something already of value."

Red watched as Neptune lingered, deep in thought. She thought about glancing at Will but was afraid of what she would find. His secret was about *her*. His *feelings* for her. Butterflies danced in the pit of her stomach and she had to force herself to focus on the main reason why they had gone there in the first place.

"Of course, it's so simple. I've got it," Neptune said, quieting the fireworks in Red's mind. *"What walks on four legs in the morning, two legs in the afternoon, and three legs in the evening?"*

Red arched a brow. "What?"

Will craned his neck to look at her. "It's a riddle," he said, and Red shot the troll a pointed look.

"So this is what Belle was talking about?"

Neptune gave a bashful smile and her gray cheeks flushed.

"What walks on four legs in the morning, two legs in the afternoon, and three legs in the evening?" Will repeated under his breath.

"Do we get a hint?" Red asked.

The troll looked at Will. "I am looking at one."

Will gulped nervously. But Red wasn't sure why. She only saw one thing when she looked at Will.

"A man?" she asked, unsure.

The troll nodded serenely. "Correct."

"Then what's the answer?" Red asked.

The troll pressed her lips together, then broke into a chuckle, unable to conceal the fun she was having. "You see, a man crawls as a baby in the morning part of life. Then on two legs in his prime, and finally with a stick in his old age."

Red rolled her eyes. "Not the answer to the riddle. The answer to our question."

"Oh, right. What's valuable to the alpha?" Neptune repeated. "There is *one* thing of much value." Her eyes moved to Will. *"I get cut but never bleed. I have teeth but never bite. Secrets I unlock, but I cannot speak. What am I?"*

"Belle wasn't kidding about the riddles."

"That one is easy," Will said, locking eyes with Neptune. "It's a key."

Neptune inclined her head and clapped. "Very good."

Red scratched her wrist and tugged on her sleeve with a frown. "There must be millions of keys in the kingdom. How can we possibly know which one to get?"

"That brings me to the final clue," Neptune said.

Red resisted the urge to groan. She had enough of these games, but they needed answers, so she forced a smile instead. "So, pray tell, where is this key?" she asked through gritted teeth.

"When his father dies, he does rise. Who am I?"

Will and Red exchanged looks. "A Prince," they said in unison.

"Prince John wears a key around his neck," Will said as if it was public knowledge. Neptune simply inclined her head.

"Wait..." Red turned to face Will. "We have to steal the key from The Prince?"

Will let out a low whistle. "That won't be easy." He bowed his head to the troll. "Thank you for your help, Neptune."

"You're very welcome, friends." She beamed. "Now you must go. The bridge will become undone soon." She walked them back out through the vines then toward the bridge.

"Oh, and one more thing…" Neptune said.

They turned around, stopping just short of the bridge. She grabbed Red's arm and pulled her down until they were at eye-level, then peered into her eyes. "The wolves… are closer than you think."

"Red, let's go," Will shouted from the bridge as it began to crumble.

Red dashed away in a hurry, and the two of them sprinted across the mountain path.

"Wait, what do you think she meant by that?" Red asked as the path twisted back and began its descent. Will shrugged, not looking back.

"Who knows, she's probably talking in riddles again."

"Will, stop." Red jumped in front of him, forcing him to look at her. The trees shielded the sunshine, and only glimmers of light illuminated his troubled face. "Are we really not going to talk about what happened?"

"*What happened* is she told us about a key which we need to steal." He tried walking around her, but she blocked his path and reached to cup his face.

"That kiss meant more to me, too," she said, searching his eyes. "Will, I've been in love with you for as long as I can remember—"

He pulled away from her affection, leaving her confused with her arms hanging in the air.

"Okay… did I miss something?" She dropped her hands. "Clearly you didn't lie because the troll would've called you out on it."

"It wasn't a lie," he assured her.

"Then what's the problem?" She tried to read his eyes, but he stared at the ground. "Is it Robin? Are you worried about what he'll think, because I'll tell you right now, I don't care—"

"It's not Robin." Will kicked a rock and turned away from her.

"Then what is it?" She took a step toward him, but he pulled back. "Will, we have always been honest with each other. Let's not change that now."

"I'm leaving, Red." He finally looked up at her, his expression hard. "As soon as I help Robin get Marian back, I'm leaving."

"Where?"

"Away from here. From this kingdom.

From these wolves. And although I do have feelings for you, and they are true, they just aren't strong enough to make me stay."

His words pierced like a dagger into her heart, deflating every inch of hope that existed in her. "Oh."

"Red—"

"No, I get it." She forced a smile as her eyes filled with tears. "I'm a big girl, Will. I can handle rejection. And yours is loud and clear."

She turned on her heels, blinking away the tears that stung her eyes. And as she marched down the mountain, she forced her mind to focus on the one thing she still had to hold on to.

Catching the alpha.

CHAPTER 8

*W*ill closed the shutters as Little John bolted the door of Robin's house. They'd have to keep their voices low so as not to be overheard. Will knew the conversation they were about to have would have them hanged if Prince John found out.

"So, did you find out what the alpha wants?" Robin asked, filling his tankard with liquor. "What do we need to do to get the mutt to give up Marian?" His dark green eyes looked from Red and narrowed on Will.

"A key," Red whispered.

Little John took a seat and leaned forward,

his eyes wide. Robin's face twisted in confusion. "What does he want with a key?"

"The troll didn't tell us, but she was confident that the alpha would do anything to get the key."

"How do we get it?" Little John asked, rubbing his beard thoughtfully.

Will joined them and perched on the edge of the small table. "That's the problem. It's highly secured," he added.

"And why is that a problem?" Robin gave him a puzzled look. "We've stolen bigger things than a key. This will be a piece of cake."

"No. Not this," Will said before gulping his drink down. His lungs burned as he slammed the tankard on the table beside him. "Prince John carries it with him at all times."

Robin's face broke into a devilish grin. He stomped his boot on the floorboards, prompting Red to shush him. A scurry of footsteps went past the front of the little house, and the group stared in silence, waiting for them to quiet.

Will turned back to Robin. "Word has it, he carries this key on a necklace."

"Right. So, we'll steal this key and then——"

"Wait," Little John said a little too loud, and everyone paused to stare at him with wide eyes. He was not usually one to speak up during these conversations, but the urgency in his voice made them pay attention. "One does not just go and steal a key from The Prince without risking getting hanged." He dragged his stubby hands across his clammy forehead. "That would be an almost impossible feat. You'd have to be the greatest thief in all the land to do it."

Robin's lips lifted into a proud grin. "Almost impossible, is still possible. Especially since *the greatest thief* is my middle name." Robin finished his drink and set his empty tankard down in triumph.

Will took the moment to glance at Red, who had been avoiding his eyes. His stomach flipped, but it was not the thought of stealing from The Prince that had him nervous. Red barely said two words to him since their encounter with the troll.

"Then we need a flawless plan," Little John whispered. "No room for mistakes."

"Worry not. I have just what we need." Robin pulled out a piece of parchment from his jacket and thrust it to Will. He opened it up to see it was an invitation.

"What is it?" Red asked, though her question was directed at Robin.

"Our dear Prince is holding a ball tomorrow night to find himself a new bride since Marian is no longer available. This invitation was inside one of the velvet bags we stole from The Prince. Here..." He threw a bag of coins to Red, who caught it. "Buy yourself a dress. Something fit for a royal."

"But I—"

Robin raised a hand. "Clothing has gone down in price. Now, the villagers are spending their last coins on food. Get something for Will too, he's going with you."

Will looked down and suppressed a smile. Even if things with Red were tense at the moment, the thought of seeing her in a dress again lit a fire inside him that was inextinguishable. But he forced himself to remain expressionless. He could see the cogs in Robin's mind turning and the formulation of a plan coming together. He was just grateful to be able to watch Red. She might not want to speak to him, but he needed to be close to her.

"Are you sure this is going to work?" Little John asked, his voice low and fearful. He wasn't wrong. If they got caught stealing from The Prince at his ball, with hundreds of guests as witnesses, they would end up at the gallows.

"If you don't want to take the risk," Robin said, putting a hand on his friend's shoulder. "I will not force you. Any of you."

Little John cast his gaze to the floor and hunched his shoulders. "Tell me the plan."

Robin squared his shoulders. "I'll give you a list of the supplies we'll need. And you'll stay with the carriage for our getaway." Robin turned to Red, his lips lifting. "I need you to distract the Prince."

"How?" she asked. Will clenched his jaw, not liking the sound of that one bit.

"Use your feminine charm. Be creative."

"Gross. That man is a snake," she retorted, but Robin wasn't listening. He turned to Will and grabbed his arm. "Stay close to her at all times. Make sure she comes to no harm."

"What are *you* going to do?" Red asked.

All eyes were on Robin as his expression turned gleeful. He pulled out a small vial from his pocket and held it up for the group to see.

"A few drops of this in Prince John's drink should do the trick. Just keep him distracted, Red. I'll take care of the rest." His words hung in the air between them, then finally Little John broke the silence.

"We're really doing this? We're going to steal from The Prince?"

Robin nodded. "You can bet your last breath we are. And then we're going to save Marian."

* * *

The next day, King Richard's castle sat gleaming in the weak sunlight, now that the blizzard had passed. Tension stiffened Will's shoulders as one of the guards looked over the carriage, the stolen invitation in his hand. The guards were not thorough enough in their search, though. For if they had checked the undercarriage, they would have found Robin. Little John sat up front, holding the reins. The guard gave a curt nod and signaled for the other guards to open the iron gates.

"Enjoy your evening, Mr. Beaumont of Nottingham," the guard said, handing the parchment back to Will. He set his jaw as he received it and forced a smile back. Tonight, he and Red were to pretend to be engaged. The proposition might have been more appealing if he hadn't messed everything up and pushed her away.

Red forced a beaming smile, resting a white-gloved hand on his arm and inclined her head so a brunette ringlet fell across her face.

The carriage stopped in front of the palace, and Will helped Red step onto a crimson carpet laid out all the way to the entrance. Now, out in the open, Red's huge navy dress was able to spill out around her. It nipped in at the waist, and the neckline curved delightfully across her collarbone, dipping low enough to make Will weak at the knees. Her red-painted lips curved upwards as her eyes flashed at him for a moment before she looked away.

She took his arm as they entered the

palace, but just as they stepped into the ball-room, surrounded by regal guests, her fingers squeezed his bicep.

"Mr. Beaumont of Nottingham," the announcer called out. Yet barely anyone bat an eyelid. A symphony of music poured from a string quartet in the far corner. The sound flooded the entire hall. Thanks to the arched ceiling offering such stunning acoustics, Will could even pick up a sniff from a gentleman by the banquet table.

Suddenly, Will imagined himself as a kid, hurrying for the food. His stomach aching unbearably. Only this time, he wore tight-fitted breeches, a fine linen shirt with ruffles at the collar, and a heavy jacket with gold stitching.

Couples danced with skirts swishing and ladies sighing. Men stood with crystal cut glasses in their hands, conversing over menial topics like the unusually early winter they were having, and how many horses they had in their collection.

Will scanned the faces in the room until he found The Prince, sticking out like a sore thumb.

"He's over there," Will muttered to Red, barely moving his lips. He watched her look over and nod while avoiding his eyes. The air shifted, and he knew Robin had snuck into the hall wearing Red's cloak. He could smell his signature scent—musty sweat mixed with liquor. Red let go of Will and made for The Prince, but Will grabbed her elbow a little too hard. Her eyes shot to him with alarm, and he loosened his grip.

"I'll be here if you need me," Will whispered. "Just twirl your hair, and I'll be right there."

Red's eyes moistened as her frown disappeared. With a nod, she turned and disappeared farther into the crowd of guests.

Will strolled over to the banquet table and looked at the piles of roasted turkey legs. There had been a shortage of poultry in the villages. Now he knew why. All of the merchants had sold their flocks to The King. Will's nostrils flared and he watched with disgust as the royal guests filled their plates, ignorant of his judgment.

"My Prince. I bid you pardon for my

intrusion. But I must thank thee for this wondrous ball."

Will's ears pricked at the sound of Red's impression of a royal. Her voice was pinched as if she had clamped her fingers over her nose. It took all of Will's resolve not to snort with laughter.

He side-stepped to get a clear look then grabbed a glass from the table, pretending to be deep in thought as the crowd parted. He caught the side profile of Red, her perfect posture emphasized her delicate curves, and her dark hair scooped up, sitting in a mass of curls atop her head. Allowing his eyes to take in the sweep of her neck, he longed to press his lips against her skin and hold her in his arms.

He drank the wine in a vain attempt to get rid of her taste which still lingered on his tongue. But who was he fooling? Nothing could ever take away the delicious taste of Red. She stood so close, yet she had become the forbidden fruit. The temptation nearly brought Will to his knees.

He gritted his teeth as he watched The Prince turn and take in the sight of Red. His gray eyes slowly dragged down her body and he flicked his tongue across his bottom lip like a predator checking out its prey.

Will set the glass down, and his hands balled into fists.

"Always a pleasure. Miss...?"

"Re—please, call me Rebecca." Red held out her gloved hand, and he took it, sliding off the glove and kissing the skin over her knuckles. Will could hear Red's heart beating rapidly as her breath hitched. He lurched forward but someone jerked on his jacket.

"Not yet," Robin hissed from behind him. Will bit his tongue and forced his hands to relax. But his fingers shook as every ounce of his body willed him to pounce on The Prince.

A lady dressed in a green gown yelped suddenly and looked crossly at the man beside her. "Keep your hands to yourself!" she warned.

The man looked at her, bewildered. "My apologies, my lady, but I have no idea what you're talking about."

Will rolled his eyes. "Behave yourself," he whispered, knowing Robin could hear him.

"Made you relax though, didn't I?" Robin

whispered back. Will could tell by the sound of his voice that he had a grin plastered on his face.

Will returned his focus back to The Prince, who had already taken the bait. "Well, Rebecca, you are quite a beauty." He led Red to a quieter corner of the hall. "Let me take a better look at you. Come on, that's it."

Red twirled elegantly on the spot, grinning at The Prince with flushed cheeks. "If I may... you are also quite easy on the eye," she replied.

The Prince was muscular and looked like his brother, only with dark, ruffled hair.

Will frowned, edging closer. The Prince was known to have many ladies on his arm. If there was one thing bigger than his castle, it was his ego. Red knew that too, and she was doing an expert job of stroking it—much to Will's dismay.

They flirted back and forth, and soon enough all the guards and guests were watching them. Will listened to Red's banter, waiting for Robin to work his magic and just spike The Prince's drink already. He wasn't sure how long he could endure watching Red cozying up to him.

"I hope I'm not too bold to say this, but I feel that I can confide in you, my Prince." The words rolled off Red's tongue in a silky tone, and this time her voice did anything but make Will laugh. He tensed and zoned in.

The Prince took a swig of his drink and set the glass down. "Of course, beautiful. But first, let us go somewhere more private." He leaned down and kissed her on the cheek, then grazed his thumb across it, cradling her face with his hands. A tiny squeak left Red's lips just as The Prince captured her with a passionate kiss.

Will wanted to transform into a wolf and tear The Prince to shreds. But he resisted and stood frozen on the spot, watching the two of them break apart and leave the hall.

Something brushed his leg. "Did you do it?" Will mumbled, inhaling Robin's scent once more.

"I gave him four drops... just to be sure. He'll be out like a light in seconds," he replied. "Now, come on. We need to be quick."

"What about the guards?" Will asked. "They're at every doorway."

"I'll handle them," Robin said. "Now, go get her. I'll be right behind you."

Will sprinted along the halls and followed the sound of Red's heartbeat. It sped up, urging Will to move faster. He reached a bolted door and rammed his shoulder into it, letting it crash to the floor. He stood in the doorway, panting and full of adrenaline, only to find The Prince lying face down on a four-poster bed. The skirt of Red's dress was just visible over the edge of it, and her stifled breaths told him she was pinned underneath the unconscious prince.

Robin came into view and raised a brow at Will as he gestured to the fallen door.

"Subtle move," he said, his voice dripping with sarcasm.

"A little help here? I can hardly breathe," Red called out. Will yanked The Prince off Red, and she slid off the bed like a cat.

"Now, he's out. I'll get the key," Robin said.

But Will couldn't take his eyes off Red. Her lipstick smeared across her cheek. He pulled out a handkerchief and dabbed the makeup off her face. She clutched his wrist, looking up at him with pleading eyes.

"Did he hurt you?" he asked, barely above a breath.

Red shook her head so fiercely, a portion of her hair fell from the back of her head and rested on her shoulder. Will lifted her face with his finger to look deeper into her eyes. He could almost taste the sweat formulating above her lip, but the way her nostrils flared told him that it wasn't The Prince who had hurt her. He had. And the sudden realization struck his heart like a dagger.

"Got it. Let's go!" Robin announced but then stopped, taking in the sight of them holding each other.

"No need to be in character right now, nobody's here," he said, then lifted the crimson hood and disappeared. Will and Red shared a sad smile, then broke apart.

Will picked up the door and leaned it against the hinges as Red fixed her hair and lipstick. All the while The Prince snored into a pillow.

"How did you knock the door off its

hinge?" she asked, looking away from the mirror.

"It must've already been broken," he said with a shrug. "Shall we get out of here?" He offered Red his arm, and she took it.

As they returned to the ballroom and made their way for the exit, no one paid any attention to them. Will and Red snuck out and rejoined Little John sitting in the front of a carriage waiting out front.

"Did you get it?" he asked eagerly. "Let me see!"

Robin reappeared and tossed John the large iron key with a grin. "Like I said... piece of cake." He climbed into the carriage, then made room for Red and Will to join him. He draped the cloak out the window and flashed his cousin a proud smile.

"You did well tonight."

Red leaned back and let out a tired breath. "I can't wait to bathe and get that man's smell off of me."

Will's lips lifted at hearing her say she didn't enjoy the kiss.

"Why aren't we moving?" Red asked.

Robin knocked on the ceiling of the carriage. "Little John, let's go!"

"Hey, Robin?" Red looked around the carriage, her voice filled with concern. "Where's my cloak?"

"It's right he—" Her cloak was gone, and his eyes shifted urgently to Will. The three of them jumped out of the carriage only to find that Little John was nowhere to be seen.

"Are you kidding me?" Robin grunted.

"I don't get it," Red said. "Why would he take off with my cloak?"

"He didn't just take your cloak," Robin hissed, kicking the wooden wheel. "That fool took the key!"

"What?" Red echoed. "What could he possibly want with the key?"

Will turned away and sniffed the air. "Whatever it is..." he said, staring in the direction Little John disappeared to. "He's headed toward The Snow Queen's castle."

CHAPTER 9

The night sky was dark with only the light of the full moon breaking through the trees. Red changed the heels for a pair of boots she had inside the carriage, which they had left midway through the woods, continuing on foot the rest of the way toward Aria's castle.

Getting that key was their only option for drawing out the alpha, then she could finally execute her long-awaited vengeance.

A howling in the distance alerted Red, and she looked at Will. The wolves were also headed to Aria's castle, and the scowl in Will's expression told her he was also surprised about the unexpected company, but he didn't look afraid.

"Looks like we're not alone." Will's voice came out in almost a growl. "Aria must've made a deal with the wolves for the key."

"And Little John was in on it!" Robin grabbed an arrow from his quiver as if reserving that one alone for Little John himself. "Wait until I get my hands on him."

"We should split up," Will suggested, moving his feet as if he couldn't wait to take off running. "I'll keep tracking Little John."

"I'll look for Aria—" Red said, but Will shook his head and gave her a concerned look.

"We should find your cloak first," he said. "You shouldn't go face to face with her without an escape plan."

"She won't hurt me."

"This isn't Aria we're dealing with," Robin added. "It's The Snow Queen, and you can leave her to *me*."

Red gave him a pointed look. "Don't hurt her."

"Sorry, Red, but it's about time somebody knocks that princess off her frozen horse." He swung on his heels and darted to the north side of the castle.

Red turned to Will and caught him sniffing the air. "What are you doing?"

"Uh, I thought I smelled something."

"Really?" She put a hand on her hip. "Let me guess, it smells like The Prince? Is that going to be a recurring joke for you now? You know what, it doesn't even matter because whomever I kiss is none of your business. And I'll have you know, I actually liked the breath of cigar and liquor."

Will's lips lifted into an amused smile as he crossed his arms. "Is that right?"

"That's right, and if he doesn't find out that it was me who stole the key from him, who knows... there may even be a second date." She turned on her heels and stomped toward the south side of the palace. It took Will a few seconds to follow, and when he did, she could sense him grinning behind her.

Eventually, he took the lead, and they came to the mouth of a tunnel. It was dark inside, and although the moon lit up the night, it only illuminated so far.

Will stepped inside without hesitation, and

Red hurried after him. "Can you see anything?" she asked, her soft voice echoing in the dark.

"I can see enough," he said, then a moment later she felt his hand grab hers, and it sent tingles up her arm. "Just stay close to me."

His skin was rough but warm, and for a moment she remembered how nice it felt against her bare leg. A wave of heat washed over her, and her face turned hot at the memory.

Will stopped, and her chest hit his back.

"What's wrong—"

"Shh…" He put a protective hand in front of her and pushed her toward the wall. Before she could scowl at him, the faint light of a torch appeared around the corner. Will crouched to the ground, pulling Red with him. He waited a few seconds then ran toward the dancing shadows on the wall. He stopped at the corner and pressed his back to the wall, keeping a protective arm across Red's chest as he waited for the person to round the corner.

Will jumped out like a predator ready to pounce on its prey, and a high-pitch scream ripped from a young woman's throat. She dropped the torch on the floor and covered her mouth.

"Wait..." Red hurried to soothe the frightened woman. Touching her shoulder, Red watched her carefully. The resemblance to Aria was remarkable. "Are you Snow? Aria's sister?"

The young woman nodded. "My sister told me to hide," she whispered as Will picked up the torch from the floor. "The wolves have invaded the castle. They keep asking for a key."

"How do you know that?" Will asked, shining the light of the fire so he could see Snow's face.

"You can communicate with animals," Red said, and Snow gave her a quizzical look.

"How do you know that?"

"Your sister told me," Red said. "Can you hear what they're saying?"

Snow nodded. "But only when they're in wolf form."

"What do you mean *wolf form*?" Red asked, looking at Snow as if she'd thrown a snowball at her face. "What other *form* do they have?"

"Human," she said, turning her attention to Will. "They're called shifters."

Red turned to Will. "Did you know about this?" she asked, but his attention had changed to something else. His eyes narrowed as he lifted the torch behind Snow.

"Will..." Before Red could say another word, Will swung his fist in the air, and a man's grunt echoed in the tunnel, followed by a loud thud. He threw the torch aside and lunged on all fours with his fists ready to swing again. Red's cloak finally came into view, revealing Little John's bloody face as Will punched once more.

"Will!" Red lunged toward him and grabbed his arm. "Enough!" Even though she wasn't stronger than him, he allowed her to push him off of Little John.

"Where's the key?" Will demanded, glaring at Little John, who by then was barely conscious.

"Aria has it," he choked out before his head fell back and he passed out.

Red sighed. "I guess he won't be of much

help," she muttered, reaching down to retrieve her cloak.

Another howl echoed in the distance, and Snow looked at Will. "You need to go," she said with a pleading expression. "You're the only one who can stop them."

Will nodded, handing Snow back the torch. "How many are there?"

"Seven, maybe ten."

"Wait, what?" Red reached for Will's arm. "You are not going out there alone."

"You heard Little John," he said, holding her gaze. "Aria has the key. Use your cloak and go steal it back. I'll distract the wolves."

She sucked in a fearful breath and peered into his hazel eyes. "Just don't do anything stupid, okay?"

He nodded, but before he walked away, he pulled her close and pressed his warm lips to her forehead. She leaned into him, feeling a blanket of warmth wash over her. He pulled back, and by the time she opened her eyes, he'd disappeared into the darkness.

Snow cleared her throat, and Red shook her head to regain her focus. "So, how do we get back into the castle?"

Snow suppressed a smile. "This way."

* * *

*P*ushing through a secret bookshelf, Red and Snow stepped out into an office, both wrapped in Red's cloak. A cracked mirror fused together by ice stood in the corner, and Red went to stand in front of it.

"Is that…?"

"The Mirror of Reason, yes," Snow replied, glancing toward their empty reflection. "Since Jack left, my sister's been locking herself in here for hours, talking to herself."

Another howl bounced off the walls, but unlike before, this wolf was close. Red reached over her quiver to touch the only arrow that mattered in that moment. The feel of its feather was rougher on the tip of her fingers, and that was by design. She needed to know which arrow to pull when she came across the alpha.

"You should go back to the tunnel," Red said, keeping her voice low. But Snow shook her head.

"I'm not hiding anymore," she said, puffing out her chest. "Someone has to stop my sister. I mean, what she did to George, and what she's been doing to the kingdom... She can't get away with it."

"I agree, but it's too dangerous. And I won't be able to keep both of us invisible with my cloak." She gave Snow an apologetic look. "Why don't you go make sure your maids are safe. They must be terrified."

"Fine," Snow grumbled, letting go of Red's cloak. "But as soon as I make sure they're safe, I'm coming back to help you."

"Deal."

Portraits rattled on the walls as Red ran toward the sound of glass shattering in the distance. Slipping on the polished floors in the oversized boots, she gritted her teeth and kept moving. But when she rounded the corner, she came to a halt as a large, gray wolf blocked her way. He was massive, almost the width of the hall. She glanced toward the window, and when she didn't see her own reflection, a wave of relief washed over there. But if she was still invisible, why was he staring her down like he could see her?

She lifted her hand slowly, reaching back for an arrow. The wolf's black eyes didn't follow her movement as she thought he might. Which meant he couldn't actually see her. He could only sense her.

She wrapped her finger around a plain arrow—no need to waste the adronna on those black eyes—and slid it carefully out of her quiver. As she nocked it in her bow, the wolf's eyes locked on hers with a snarl.

She drew the arrow back, but before she could release it, the wolf's claws were already knocking her bow from her hands and pinning her to the floor. Her hood fell back and she appeared into sight, trapped underneath his massive paw.

He growled in her face, his large teeth inches from her cheek. She turned her face away from the smell of wet grass and dog breath. Her eyes landed on the scattered arrows on the floor. If she could reach just one, she could dig it into his neck. But it was as if the wolf could hear what she was thinking because he put more of his weight on top of her, and she could barely breathe.

"Hey!" Snow's voice barked from the end

of the hall, and the wolf looked up at her.
"Let go of my friend."

Red cocked her head just enough to see
Snow holding Red's bow with an arrow ready
to be released. The wolf made a low guttural
growl, and Red twisted her face as hot drool
dripped on her cheek.

Oh. Gross.

"If you're not going to hurt her, then why
are you still holding her down?" Snow replied,
looking at the wolf.

He snarled again, and Snow pulled back
the arrow.

"I'm going to count to three," she said
firmly. But the wolf didn't move.

"One…"

Red threw her head back, looking at a
Snow upside down.

"Two…"

But then her eyes locked on the black tip
of the arrow. The final one laced with black
adronna. Red gasped. "Snow, don't—"

"Three!"

The wolf lunged at Snow just as she shot
the arrow. He hit the floor with a loud thud,
and Red jumped to her feet. He staggered to

his paws, whimpering as the black arrow stuck out from his shoulder. He whimpered and sprinted down the hall but wobbled as his limbs went numb. He stumbled on a jumbled rug and fell through the window, shattering the glass with a loud clang.

Red ran to the window and spotted the wolf lying, paralyzed on the grass, twenty feet below, next to the frozen lake. Ice monsters roared as they marched in the yard, swinging their fists toward more wolves.

"He's hurt, but he's still alive," Snow said, coming to stand next to Red.

She wanted to punch her fist through a wall. The only black arrow she had left was wasted on that meaningless wolf. But then her thoughts were ripped back by the howling of all the wolves together. It traveled in the night like a warning siren.

"What's happening?" she asked, looking at Snow.

"The alpha is here," Snow whispered.

"The alpha?" Red's brows shot up. "Where?"

Snow closed her eyes as if trying to distinguish one voice from the many inside her head. "Going for Aria in the coronation hall—"

Red threw the hood over her head and took off running, picking up a handful of arrows on the way.

"Red, wait!"

No. She was done waiting. The alpha was there, and she was not going to let him get away again.

A blast of ice came at Red as soon as she stepped out onto the balcony overlooking the main hall. She slid on the floor until her feet hit the wooden railing.

While still on the floor, she spotted Aria standing only a few feet to her left, shooting daggers of ice at the wolves below. The roar of an ice monster was cut short as a brown wolf lunged at it and bit off its head. The monster crumbled into a pile of snow, and the massive, muscular wolf lifted his eyes to glare at Aria.

Red gasped as his *amber eyes* glowed like the sun. That was him. The wolf she'd seen outside her window the day her Grams died. She fumbled with the loose arrows, but her hand was shaking so much, she had to ball them into fists to regain her composure.

Aria turned in Red's direction, even though she was invisible, and cocked her head. "Ry, are you up there?" Aria asked.

"No." Snow appeared at the door and stepped in front of Red. "It's me."

"I told you to hide," Aria said angrily.

The wolf snarled from down below, and Red jumped to her knees, setting her bow and arrow in place.

"He wants the key you stole," Snow replied, interpreting the wolf's thoughts. "And he's not leaving without it."

Aria flashed him a wicked grin. "Is that right? And if I don't?"

The wolf growled so loudly, the ground shook under Red's knees. She lifted her bow and aimed at his head. Even though her hands were still shaking, it would be hard to miss because this wolf was larger than the gray one she encountered earlier.

"This key does not belong to you." Aria lifted the rustic iron key, and guilt tugged at

Red's conscience. She could easily sneak down and take it from Aria's hand, but she couldn't risk losing the opportunity to kill the wolf. This was the moment she'd been waiting for since she was twelve, and now she had the perfect shot.

She sucked in a breath, hands slowly steadying against her bow. Then closing one eye, she aimed the arrow at his neck. This was it. He was finally going to pay for what he did.

"You're not a killer, Will. So stop acting like one." Aria brushed it off, but it took several seconds for Red's brain to process the name Aria just said.

Did she just call the wolf Will?

The wolf stepped forward, tossing his head and looking from Snow to Aria as if having a conversation.

"He wants to know why you're helping the alpha when he took Marian?" Snow interpreted.

"If you were still part of the pack, I guess you would know," Aria said bitterly. "But since that's not the case... why don't you go on back to your job as Robin's personal tracker."

Red couldn't breathe.

She dropped her bow and noticed as the wolf's eyes turned in her direction. His expression shifted from anger to fright as his gaze locked with hers.

The swoosh of an arrow flew over her head followed by a yelp from Aria. Red whipped around and spotted the large iron key pierced to the wall.

Robin.

But Red couldn't move. It was as if a black arrow pierced her heart and paralyzed her from head to toe. All she could do was stare at the key a few feet away, unable to move.

Another wave of howling shot in the air, and Aria began shooting ice daggers again. In the blink of an eye, Snow snatched the key from the wall and descended the steps to the hall, but before she could run away with it, a large golden-colored wolf landed in front of her.

The howling fell to a deafening silence, and Snow gasped.

That was the alpha.

Snow moved away until her back pressed against the stair railing. The alpha had her cornered, but why didn't Aria step in to defend her sister? Had she become *that* evil?

Suddenly, the alpha bowed its head, and Snow cocked hers, her frightened expression changing into a frown. When the alpha opened its mouth, Snow willingly placed the key under his tongue.

The golden wolf bowed his head again as if it were a gesture of gratitude, then turned around and howled to the winds. The pack followed in unison, and a minute later they were all gone.

All...but one.

CHAPTER 10

*W*ill knew he needed to move, but he froze under Red's piercing gaze. She had him trapped, as if her eyes had the power to control him against his will. Any hope that she might not have seen him transform were dashed, the hurt and devastation was all over her face.

She blinked, breaking the spell she had over him, and the alpha's scent was growing faint. He bounded for the front of the castle and descended the steps four at a time.

He thought if he could get to the alpha, convince him to release Marian, then Red might not look at him like a traitor. But deeper into the forest, the scent was scattered. He followed several leads, but they ran cold. He growled with frustration and sniffed the air. The trail was gone.

He turned back to the castle but looked up at the glittering peaks rising out of the forest and considered whether he should even go back. Once Red told Robin who Will was—*what* he was—he would never accept him.

But as he padded further on, a familiar scent took over his senses, mingled with the metallic taste of blood. He raced through the trees and stopped at the edge of the forest.

In an instant, he transformed back into human form and crouched to retrieve his clothes from inside a hedge. He returned to the castle grounds to find Robin securing one of the horses. He looked up as Will approached and raised his hand with his index finger and thumb pinched.

"We were *this* close to the alpha. This close. And now he has the blasted key," Robin said as Red approached from the castle. Despite his discontented words, he patted a bundle of blankets on the back of his horse and looked triumphant. "But no matter. We have a new bargaining chip."

Will rounded the horse and stepped closer to take a look. Under the pile of blankets was a tuft of blonde hair. A steady drip of blood stained the grass, and a pair of dark eyes stared at him, stunned.

"Levi," he whispered under his breath.

"Don't get too close," Robin warned. "It's a you-know-what."

"A wolf," Red said firmly. Will straightened and looked up at her, standing a few feet away, keeping space between them. Her hand rested on the hilt of her knife.

"What are we going to do with him?" Will asked, trying to keep his voice steady.

"He's paralyzed... for now. So, we'll take him back to the safe house and get a word to the alpha that if he wants his dog back, he'll need to give us Marian," Robin spat the words as if every syllable were poison.

Will took a step forward. "And Little John?" he asked, studying Robin's expression. His face twisted in disgust at the sound of the traitor's name.

"He's dead to me. He can stay here and

rot in the dungeon for all I care. I may be a lot of things, but I'm not a fool. Anyone who lies to me is going to pay the price."

Will stared at Red, wondering why she hadn't told Robin the truth.

"I'll take him back," Will said. "Who knows how long the paralysis will last. We need to lock him up somewhere secure."

"You're not going alone," Red said firmly. "Robin, why don't you talk to Snow and send an owl to the alpha."

"Snow, who?" Robin asked. "Aria's sister?"

"Yes. Snow can communicate with animals. She'll know what to do."

Will looked at her with pleading eyes, begging for her forgiveness, but she avoided looking in his direction. Robin thought on her words for a moment, then Red lifted her hood and disappeared. The sound of her footsteps grew quieter as she headed further into the forest.

Robin lifted a brow. "What's wrong with her?"

Will did his best impression of a nonchalant shrug. "She's probably upset seeing Aria like that. I'll go and talk to her."

Robin gave a nod, and Will made no hesitation as he ran after Red.

Red stood, her hood down, on the riverbank. Will picked up the salty scent of her tears and noticed her shoulders quivering underneath her thick cloak.

Will placed a hand on her shoulder, and in an instant, she turned toward him with her bow and arrow ready to shoot. Her shiny face twisted into a scowl as she stepped back, aiming the arrow toward his chest.

"Turn into a wolf right now," she demanded through gritted teeth.

Will lifted his hands slowly. "Red—"

"Shift, now!" She pulled the arrow back further with shaky hands. "Don't make me say it again."

"No." His voice was soft but firm, and he dropped his hands. "If you want to kill me, you're going to have to do it like this, because *this* is who I am, Red. I'm a human with feelings just like you."

"You are nothing like me." The tears streaming down her cheeks tortured Will's soul. "You're a killer. This whole time. It was you," she said between sobs. "How did I not see it?"

"I didn't kill your grand—"

"Don't you dare even mention her," Red said acidly. Thick clouds cast them into a darkness to match the color of Red's mood.

"I didn't kill her." He pushed through the lump in his throat.

Red's breath hitched and she shook her head. "Don't lie to me. I saw you that day. Outside the house. You were there as a... wolf." She choked on the last word and pressed her eyes shut as if trying to keep the pain at bay.

"Yes, I was there. And yes, as a wolf." Finally saying the words to her unleashed a tightness that had been in his chest for so long, that despite her reaction, a part of him was relieved. No more lies. "But only because I heard you scream, and I could smell the blood. I *stayed* to keep you safe in case the killer came back. That's why you saw me."

Red lowered her bow slowly, but her hard expression made it clear she did not put down the defenses. "You know who the killer is?"

Will shook his head, deflated. "I tried following his trail but... I wasn't a good tracker at fifteen."

Her shoulders sagged, and she dropped her hands. The bow and arrow fell to the ground. "You still lied to me..." she cried. "All these years, full of lies."

Will's insides squirmed again, and he clenched his teeth. "I'm so sorry that I've kept this from you, but I was so scared of losing you." He stepped forward and took her hands. When she didn't pull away, a glimmer of hope lifted his heart. "Red, I have loved you since I was fifteen years old. Since the first time I saw you apple picking by the waterfall. My love for you has never been a lie."

"Your *love* for me?" Her look of confusion turned into anger, throwing Will off guard. She shoved him with both hands. "If you truly loved me, you wouldn't have made a fool out of me this whole time." She thumped her fists against his hard chest, and though the impact was like that of a small child, her cries pierced into his heart like a dagger. Any glimmer of hope that Red could forgive him was dashed and he watched, with devastation as she sobbed in front of him.

He gently took Red's arms. "I'm sorry."

Red wrenched her arms away from his grip and pulled back. The moonlight illuminated her face, the look of incredulity in plain view. "I can't," she breathed, exhausted. "I can't *ever* forgive you for this."

Will's insides writhed like a pit of snakes. He bit back against tears, furious with himself and crushed by her words. He was a fool to believe she would ever look at him the same way. Now, he was one of *them*. And yet, he wasn't. He'd been banished from his pack, and now rejected from the one person he truly loved. Now, he belonged to no one.

"There you are," Robin said brightly as he emerged from the tree line. "I stole some food from the kitchen on my way out." He padded the sheepskin sack hanging from the saddle of his horse and smiled, apparently not aware he had walked into something.

"Right," Red said in a raspy voice as she wiped her face. "We need to get this *mutt* back to the village." Without another word, she marched back toward the carriage.

Robin watched her walk away then elbowed Will in the ribs. "Well done, you always manage to cheer her up."

Will chuckled, but what he really wanted to do was cry. He was going to miss Robin. He'd been like an older brother to Will for many years, but there was no more hiding. He needed to be the one to tell Robin the truth. He owed him that much.

But first, he needed to make sure Levi was out of danger.

* * *

*N*ight fell as they returned to the village. An orange glow flooded the sky above, and the sound of many voices filled the air. Will and Robin exchanged looks. It seemed The Prince had already noticed someone had stolen his key.

"Getting to the safe house unnoticed will be a challenge. The square is teeming with guards," Robin said thoughtfully.

He was right. Will looked at Levi slumped over the back of Robin's horse and chewed his lip. If anyone were to see them like this, ques-

tions would be asked, and when they discovered Levi, and recognized Robin—a wanted
thief—they would be hanged at dawn.

"We can take him to my place?" Will
offered. "It's away from the square, and we
can tie him up in the cellar."

Robin clapped his shoulder. "Great plan.
We'll go and deal with the dog. And Red, why
don't you—" Robin stopped, noticing that she
was no longer with them. "She's always
running off. Maidens, am I right?" He rolled
his eyes with a humored grin. Apparently
nothing was going to squash his happy mood
now that they had the collateral he wanted.

Will tied the horses to a post outside the
back of his home. It sat nestled in a row of
small houses, and the little pockets of land
behind each dwelling barely offered enough
room for a horse to turn around before the
next row of houses.

Will unbolted his door and it creaked
open. He lit a lantern as Robin carried Levi's
immobile body over his shoulder.

They were careful to make minimal noise
as they made their way down to the cellar, so
as not to arouse suspicion from the neighbors.

But Will did not think it mattered much. The Millers next door were in their eighties and turned in for the night before dark. The Blacksmiths, on the other side, worked through the night.

"It's freezing down here," Robin grumbled. Will lit another lamp, gold flames licked the stone walls and shone light over the large makeshift bed in the corner of the room.

"Why is there a bed down here?" Robin asked as he lowered Levi to it.

"I like how cool it is during the summer," Will said.

Robin looked at him with mild suspicion but then shook his head.

"Are any of these bottles full, or have you drunk all the wine?" Robin grabbed a dark glass and peered into it with squinted eyes.

"So, what's the plan here?" Will asked, turning to Robin.

"What do you mean?" Robin looked up from the glass. "We set up a trade with the alpha. The mutt for Marian."

"And if the alpha doesn't agree with the trade?" Will asked.

"What makes you think he wouldn't agree?"

"Because wolves communicate telepathically, and I'm pretty sure that although this wolf can't move, he's already tried reaching out to his pack with his mind," Will explained. "And if the alpha didn't come for him while we were on the road, I'm not so sure he cares that we have him at all."

Robin put the glass back on the table with a scowl. "And how on earth would you know all of this?"

Will sucked in a breath, bracing himself. This was it. The time to come clean to Robin. "I know all this because—"

"Will," Red's voice entered his mind. Will fell silent and focused on her voice, frozen at the sound. "Will, come to the square. Now."

Will looked up at Robin. "Something's wrong." He bolted up the stairs and barely took a breath as he headed for the square. Robin appeared to his left, running with his bow in hand, gripping it so tightly, his knuckles were turning white.

"Did you hear that?" he asked as they ran side by side. "I heard screams."

They entered the square to find a convoy of guards. A line of black horses with guards stood to the side as the sheriff wrestled with a young woman, his blade pressed up to her throat.

Even at the distance Will knew who it was. He eyed her dark braid resting on her shoulder and her oversized boots sagging at her narrow calves.

"Let go of her," Robin barked, raising his bow and aiming an arrow at the sheriff.

He gave a hearty laugh. "Now, now. You don't want to try anything foolish." He yanked on Red, pressing the blade to her skin, prompting Robin to drop his bow and raise his hands.

"All right, all right," he said, his voice rising in panic. Two guards roughly grabbed them and pushed them to join the sheriff.

"You have something that does not belong to you," the sheriff snarled. Will grimaced against the stench of liquor and tobacco on his breath. "Give me the key. Now."

Robin shook his head. "We don't have it."

The sheriff stared him down, trying to read him. "You don't? We'll see about that."

He yelled out a command, and every guard in the square struck a match in unison and raised their flaming arrows to the sky. Will and Robin staggered back, looking around them. "It's your choice, *Robin Hood.* Give back the key or watch your village burn... again."

Will swallowed nervously and watched Robin, hoping he had another trick up his sleeve to get them out of this mess. But this time, Robin stood immobile and ashen-faced.

"I don't have it *anymore*," he said, almost pleading.

A group of men pushed their way into the square. One of them wrestled with a guard, and a flaming arrow sailed through the sky and landed on a hay bale in the back of a carriage. The hay exploded into flames and signaled the start of chaos.

"Stop fighting, stand your ground," Robin barked at the men.

But the villagers didn't listen. Will didn't blame them. These men were not willing to stand by and watch their village burn again. And neither could Will. He rammed his shoulder into the chest of a nearby guard, then caught the arrow before it fell and extinguished the flame.

A huge fight broke out as the men fought with the guards. Arrows flew across the square and rooftops set ablaze. Will knocked out a guard who was pounding his fist into the chest of a fallen man, while Robin shot an arrow. It landed in the back of a guard who was just about to cut down a villager with his sword.

"Watch out!" Will called to Robin as a metal arm wrapped around his neck. But then a shadowy figure appeared, and Robin's attacker fell in a heap on the floor. Will kicked a guard down and raced to Robin's side just as the shadowy figure stepped into the light. Dancing flames illuminated his face.

"Little John. You *traitor*," Robin said vehemently. He grabbed his shirt and scowled. "Give me one good reason why I shouldn't thrust this knife between your eyes."

"I can explain everything," he said. Their conversation broke as two guards descended on them. Screams filled the air, and the stench of burning wood choked in the back of Will's throat.

Red's scream shot like an arrow straight to

his heart. He followed the sound and caught sight of her bundled in the back of a carriage with the sheriff. The driver yelled at the horses, and in a moment, the carriage rolled away from the burning square.

Will left Robin and Little John fighting with the guards and tried to block out the sounds of swords clashing, bones crunching, and coughing. He raced in the direction of the carriage, but as he left the square, the carriage had already gone into the forest.

In an instant, Will transformed into a wolf and ran as fast as his four legs would carry him, following Red's scent. He rounded a corner to find the carriage moving far too quickly across the uneven path. Red shrieked and Will bounded forward. Once beside the carriage, he dipped his head and rammed his shoulder into it, causing it to fall on its side with a crash.

Will bit the door and ripped it off its hinges, spitting it across the path. The horses neighed as the driver hopped down and ran into the dark forest.

The sheriff stumbled out, blood trickling down his neck from a gash cut cleanly across his cheek. His eyes widened as he took in the sight of the wolf towering above him, baring his fangs with a deep growl.

"Easy," he said in a wavering voice. "Easy boy." He staggered away from the carriage and ran into the forest with a wail.

Confident the sheriff was not going to return, Will turned his attention to the carriage. Red emerged and stumbled out. Will sniffed her and looked for signs that she was hurt. Red pushed his snout away.

"I'm fine, Will," she said.

Will stepped back and let his tail wag but stopped at Red's frown.

"Go back to your pack. You don't belong here."

Will whimpered despite himself. When in wolf form, he had less control over his natural urges. Red unfastened one of the horses from the carriage.

"Don't follow me."

Will watched her climb onto the horse and give him a wary look before she kicked. The horse bolted, and all Will could do was whine.

Will, help me.

Will snapped out of his thoughts at Levi's

cry. The sound of his coughing had him on alert, and he jumped into action.

* * *

*U*pon his return, Will found his house with black smoke billowing out from the roof. Most of the village had now been set alight, and women and children ran away, frantic.

Will, still in his wolf form, burst through the back door and rushed down the steps of the cellar. Gray smoke filled the room, and he tried to ignore the urge to cough as the swirling smoke entered his lungs.

Levi lay on the bed in human form, weakly moving. Though the effect of the adronna plant was wearing off, he still couldn't run. He coughed and gasped, struggling to catch his breath.

Will bit Levi's cloak and pulled him out of the house. Levi retched onto the grass and took greedy gulps of air. Though it was not much clearer outside.

Will picked him up and ran to the edge of the woods, propping Levi up against a tree.

Back in the forest, the air was cleaner and Will took deep breaths to clear his lungs.

Levi shakily got to his feet and shifted back into his wolf form. He shook his body like a dog, relieved to be getting back his mobility. Relief washed over Will at seeing that Levi was all right and back on his feet. Levi puffed air from his snout.

Come with me, Will. I'll tell the alpha you saved my life.

Will was tempted by the idea. But as he looked back at the burning village, he caught sight of a child standing in a top window of a house on fire.

I can't leave them, but you should go.

Will charged for the house and broke through the downstairs window without another thought. Black smoke flooded his vision and choked his lungs, but he pressed on, climbing up the stairs and sniffing for the child. A piece of roof fell to the floor, and a line of fire separated him from the room. He dashed forward, growling against the heat, and found the little boy huddling in the corner. Will ignored the look of terror on his face and crashed his shoulder into the wall, a section of rocks crumbled away, opening a gap just big enough to jump through. Will crouched and bowed his head. The boy tumbled forward, climbing onto his back and clutching his fur with tiny hands.

Hoping the boy wouldn't let go, he jumped down just as the fire exploded, pushing them farther into the path. Will took the boy to the square, following the sound of a mother screaming for her son. Red stood afar off, guiding the villagers to safety.

The boy wriggled from Will's back and reached out his hands, running into the arms of a woman who cried at the sight of him.

"My baby! I'm never letting you go again!"

Robin, along with the men in the village, attacked the last of the guards as the whole village burned to ashes. But Will had no time to watch as he heard more cries from people still stuck in their homes.

Will darted in and out of buildings, his sensitive paws stinging and the ends of his fur searing. But he paid no attention. Running on pure adrenaline, he rescued more women and children and took them to the group settled next to Red.

He laid an elderly woman on the ground, unconscious. Red hurried over and kneeled beside her.

Will ran back to the last cry, coming from the final house he had not searched. A little girl with fiery red hair sobbed and coughed as she cowered in a wooden closet. There was not even an inch of floor that was not on fire. Will winced against the pain and roared, throwing all his weight against a wall. Once inside, he wrenched open the closet with his claws and grabbed the young girl's dress between his teeth.

The entire roof collapsed moments after they were freed from the house, and Will limped across the square, the girl hanging from his mouth as he brought her to Red.

Embers of fire burned within his fur, and each step was like standing on a bed of knives. But as he approached Red, the villagers stood stunned, staring at him with a mixture of fear and gratitude.

Red took the little girl in her arms, but her eyes kept locked with Will's.

"Thank you," she whispered, her face softening.

Will's heart swelled, and in that moment, it didn't matter that she hated him, or that he stood in wolf form amidst the villagers. All he wanted to be was a protector. To keep people safe. If he had not been in wolf form, he would have offered a smile. Will considered whether to muster one, but then he saw a reflection in Red's eyes as she looked past him with a gasp.

"No!"

A deep ache spread from the back of his shoulder and pierced a nerve. Will howled and turned back to see Robin standing in the distance. Another arrow poised, aiming for him.

Will forced himself up on his paws and ran into the forest. Another arrow whistled in the air and pierced into his ribcage. He howled again, this time with a whimper as the pain shot up his spine. He ran as fast and as hard as his body would allow, but the taste of blood overwhelmed him. He slowed and slumped to the ground, panting as the pain intensified.

A twig snapped in the distance, followed

by another. Will sniffed, but his mouth filled with blood and the smell was too strong to sense whatever was approaching.

Moments later, an entire pack of wolves surrounded him... fangs bared.

CHAPTER 11

a baby's cry floated above their heads like a constant wail in the wind. The villagers camped by the edge of the forest and spoke in dull tones as they looked at their burning homes with despair. Their whole lives gone in one night.

But Red had bigger worries. She chewed her lip and clutched the hilt of her knife as she watched the dark forest, waiting for Will to reappear. He was injured. He had to come back.

"I was told a wolf saved my life," the older woman who had been unconscious touched Red's hand. Red shook her head, shifting her focus back to the woman's injured leg.

"It's true." Red offered the woman a soft smile as she wrapped her injured leg. "He saved a lot of lives today."

"I guess they're not all bad like we thought, huh."

"No, they're not." Red's eyes flickered from the woman's leg to the woods where Will had disappeared to. Why hadn't he shifted into human form and returned to the village already?

"You!" Robin's voice came out as a growl. "You've got some nerve coming back here."

Red jumped to her feet and hurried to stand next to her cousin.

"I never left, Robin," Little John said with a frown. "I only made a deal with Aria to get the information I knew you wanted."

Robin balled his fists and clenched his jaw, ready to knock him out. But Little John lifted his arms defensively.

"I know where Marian is."

Robin's eyes widened, and for a moment he didn't seem to be breathing. "You better not be lying to me."

"I'm not. I swear," Little John assured him. "Aria told me in exchange for the key."

"And how do you know she wasn't lying to you?"

"Because she doesn't care what happens to Marian," Little John explained. "She had her own reasons for trading the key with the wolves."

"Which are?"

"She didn't tell me."

"What was that key even for?" Red chimed in.

"I don't know that either, but none of that matters." He looked at Robin again. "We finally know where Marian is. Isn't that all you cared about?"

Robin narrowed his eyes. "Where is she?"

Little John swallowed hard. "I do have one request," he said in a strangled voice.

"Don't bargain with me, you fool," Robin spoke through gritted teeth.

"I'm not. I just have nowhere else to go," Little John pleaded with a frown. "My brother is here, Robin. I want to return."

"Fine." Robin balled his fists again. "You can return to your family. Now, tell me where she is before I lose my patience."

"She was last seen in Pearl Island," Little

John finally said. "It's just off the coast of the King of the Shores' territory. If we catch a boat at Pirate's Cove, we'll arrive at the island within a few hours."

"Great, let's gather the people," Robin called out, turning to Red. "We head west tonight." It took Red a few seconds to realize he was talking to her.

"Wait, now?" she asked, and he looked at her like she sprouted two heads.

"Of course, now. The village just burned to ashes, and the people are hungry. The sooner we get to a neighboring village, the better." Robin paused and looked around for a moment. "Where the heck is Will? We'll need all the help we can get."

Red opened her mouth to tell Robin the truth about Will, but then her cousin's face darkened as he cast his gaze to the ground. He hunched as if the weight of the whole world rested on his shoulders. The last thing he needed was to deal with yet another betrayal.

Red closed her mouth and let out a long sigh.

"Hey." Robin grabbed her arms as if to steady her. "Everything is going to be fine.

We've rebuilt our lives from the ashes before, and we're going to do it again."

She nodded. "I know."

He lifted her chin with his knuckles, and she smiled.

"All right. I'll go find Will and we'll meet you at Egret village. That's the next village west."

"Where do you think he is?" Robin asked, concern showing in his expression for the first time. "The mutt is gone. Do you think he did something to Will?"

"I think Will can handle himself just fine," she assured him. "I'll find him, and we'll catch up with you in no time. You should let Little John help."

"I'll think about it. Now, hurry up." Robin nudged her. "If you're not at Egret village by morning, I'm leaving to get Marian without you."

Red leaned in and gave her cousin a tight hug. Just in case she came face to face with the wolves and never made it back. She pulled back and rushed away before Robin could see the tears welling up in her eyes.

She ran back into the village and found

the horses still tied up near Will's house. Luckily, they had been secured far enough away from the homes that caught on fire.

"Hey, girl." She brushed Scout's mane and nuzzled her face. "I need you to go with Robin for now, okay?" She untied her along with Robin's horse and watched as they galloped toward where Robin was. Then she turned around and looked at Pedigree. "As for you…" she said, undoing the knot on the rope. "You're going to take me to Will. Can you do that?" Pedigree licked her hand, and she smiled. "Good, then let's go find him."

* * *

*R*ed tightened her cloak around herself to block out the chill of the dark night. It had been almost an hour of riding in what felt like circles, yelling Will's name, and still nothing.

What if the wolves took him? What if they killed him?

Her eyes filled with tears, but she wiped them away in frustration. She shouldn't have been crying for him. He lied to her. He betrayed her. She wanted him gone. She even told him to leave. Then why was the thought of him really being gone so excruciating? Everything inside her ached.

Pedigree sprinted into a clearing, and Red's heart leapt with renewed hope. She galloped to the center of a meadow, but Red still saw nothing. "Will!" she yelled for the thousandth time, but there was no answer.

Pedigree sniffed the ground, and Red craned her neck. Though it was dark, the bright light of the moon illuminated a body covered in snow a few feet away, his black hair a direct contrast to the whiteness around him.

"Will!" Red jumped down from the horse and rushed to Will's side. She dug him out and turned him over. The snow beneath him turned crimson from the blood oozing from a gash under his ribcage. Red's stomach churned.

"Will, wake up!" She lifted his head and slapped his face gently. His lips had turned blue, and her eyes filled with tears. "Will, please wake up." At noticing he wasn't wearing any clothes, Red removed her cloak as quickly as she could and wrapped it around him, but he was going to need a lot more heat than that. "I need to get you out of here."

She wrapped her arms around his torso and pushed herself to her feet, straining against his dead weight. "Come on, Will."

She tried pulling him up again, but he was too heavy for her. The horse came over and nuzzled Will's hair.

"Okay, Pedigree. Stay still. I'm going to try putting him on you."

She moved to stand behind Will and hooked her arms under his armpits. Once secured, she dragged him to the side of the horse. But as she noticed the distance it would take to lift him up, her heart sank. His all-lean-muscled body was too heavy for her to lift.

"No!" she yelled at the universe. "He can't die!"

Tears slid down her cheeks, and she laid him back down. "I'm sorry," she cried, lifting his head and putting it on her lap. "I'm not strong enough. I'm so sorry." She hugged his head and kissed his forehead. "And I'm sorry for what I said. You do belong with us. You always have. Please, Will. Please, open your eyes." She caressed his cheek. "I need you."

A whimper came from behind her, and she turned her head to find a pair of bright gray eyes staring back at her. She gasped and jumped to her feet. Swinging around, she pulled out her knife and pointed at the huge wolf in front of her. It was the same wolf she had paralyzed back at Aria's castle, which meant it was the same wolf they took to the cellar.

"You are not taking him," she said, wiping the tears from her eyes with the back of her free hand. "Now, go away. Leave us alone."

The wolf's eyes fell to almost a frown, then he bowed his head and lowered his whole body to the ground. Another whimper escaped his mouth, and he looked up at her.

She lowered her knife then glanced at Pedigree. She hadn't moved or run away. She wasn't scared of the wolf, which explained why she and Will got along so well. Red turned back to the wolf, and their eyes locked again.

"If you can carry him, blink twice."

The wolf blinked twice, and a wave of relief washed over Red. She stepped aside and watched as the young wolf walked away then came back with a pile of clothes in his mouth. He then nuzzled his way underneath Will's body, throwing him gently onto his back. Once he stood, he turned east before glancing at Red.

"No," Red said. "We're not going back to the village." She mounted Pedigree then turned to the young wolf. "Follow me."

* * *

The first place Red thought of hiding was at Aria's tree. At first glance, it looked like a simple tree burrow, but underneath, Aria had made herself a home. That was where Aria lived after she left Sherwood. Red had spent many nights there with Aria, hiding from The Queen and talking about the mirror shards. At one point, Aria had even shown the incomplete mirror to Red. This would be the perfect place to hide Will until he could heal. Otherwise, Robin would figure out that he was the wolf he'd shot with his arrow, and maybe even try to finish him off in a blind rage.

She dismounted then rushed to push aside

the piece of wood that covered the opening of the burrow. By the time she turned around, the young wolf had already lowered himself to the ground so Red could reach for Will. Once she hooked her hands under his arms, the wolf stood, using the momentum to nudge Will into Red's arms. She strained all her muscles under his weight, but she was able to at least stay on her feet. The young wolf walked around the tree then came back as a young man, combing his blond hair, pulling up his pants, and slipping on his shirt.

"Let me help you," he said, grabbing Will's legs.

They entered carefully into the hole at the bottom of the tree bark, then slowly descended the small steps made of tree roots until they reached a ground floor. There was just enough room for a small bed and a wooden table with a cabinet sitting on top. Piles of books and papers scattered across the earth floor, and the table had wooden bowls and cups stacked up. *The place once had walls of ice, but the memory of Aria and her powers was long gone,* Red thought as she glanced at the tree roots and muddy walls.

They lowered Will's body onto a blanket on the floor, and after removing the blood-soaked cloak from him, Red hurried to cover his body with another blanket. She tossed her cloak aside then looked up at the young man.

"What's your name?"

"Levi."

"Levi..." She pointed across the room. "Can you look in that cabinet over there for a dark green jar?"

He did as he was told and scanned through the labels. "Got it." By the time he brought it to her, she had Will's open wound exposed and ready.

"What is it?" Levi asked.

"Poultice," she said, scooping it from the jar and examining the open wound for another moment. "Can you get a clean rag from that cabinet too, please?"

Levi came back with a few rags just as she finished covering the wound with the moist mass. She grabbed the rag and placed it over the open wound to concentrate the remedy.

"Is he going to be okay?" Levi asked, his voice shaky.

"Depends who's asking," Red replied with

an edge in her voice. "Just tell your alpha he's dead and leave him alone."

"The alpha doesn't want him dead."

"Then why would he leave Will on that field to bleed out?"

"Will's been banished, and the pack is very particular about that," Levi explained. "Still, the alpha sent me back to help him. To help *you*."

Red looked up at Levi for the first time since they'd arrived. "How did he know I was coming?"

"We can smell you from miles away."

Red shifted her attention back to Will. Everything was making sense now. His expertise in tracking and in finding her even when she was invisible.

Grabbing another scoop of the poultice, she rubbed it over the burns on his shoulder and down his arm.

"You said Will was banished," she said, her voice soft. "What did he do?"

Levi hesitated, but only for a moment. "He disobeyed the alpha's order, and it got his brother killed."

Red looked up, shocked. "What? The alpha killed his brother just because Will disobeyed him? What kind of monster leads you?"

"No, it wasn't like that. Will's brother *was* the alpha at the time," Levi explained. "And in trying to save Will, he got killed."

"Wait…" Red shook her head. "Will's brother was an alpha?"

Levi nodded. "And a very good one."

Red frowned, still rubbing his shoulder. "What about the alpha you have now? Who is he?"

"We're sworn to secrecy when it comes to the identity of the pack," Levi said. "Especially the alpha."

When he said nothing else, Red looked up at him with a frown. "I'm sorry we paralyzed you and took you captive."

He shrugged. "I knew Will wouldn't let anything happen to me." His eyes shifted back to an unconscious Will. "He's always looked out for me."

Red lifted the rag and examined his wound again. "It doesn't seem to be getting any better."

"Maybe I should go get his sister," Levi said.

Red's eyes widened in shock. "Belle knows he's a wolf?"

Levi nodded. "And this isn't the first time Will's been injured like this. Wolves get hunted all the time. His sister has treated pretty much the whole pack by now."

Red nodded, remembering Belle had said she found Will's brother injured from a wolf trap, and that was how they met. "But how will she get here? It's a two day journey to her place."

Levi offered a small smile. "I can run fast. Really fast."

Red couldn't help but smile at his humble-brag. It reminded her of Will when she first met him. "Okay, go." She padded Will's sweaty forehead with another rag. "And please hurry. I don't know how much longer he'll last."

* * *

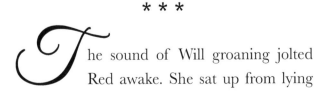he sound of Will groaning jolted Red awake. She sat up from lying

next to him and dabbed his forehead with the rag, then his neck. He wasn't sweating as much anymore, which was a good sign.

"Will?" She touched his forehead with the back of her hand. His temperature wasn't as high anymore. "Can you hear me?"

She lifted the blanket carefully until she could see his wound again. The poultice had dried, and the open gash was finally closed. She had never seen someone heal so fast, but maybe it was a wolf thing.

"Why are you peeking under the covers?" Will muttered, and she looked up at him as a wave of relief washed over her. Not only was he alive, but he was teasing her. She dropped the blanket with a smile.

"There you are." She reached to caress his face, brushing a strand of his hair off his eyes. "You scared me there for a second."

She offered him her sheepskin flask and watched him drink.

He grimaced. "Why did you come back for me?" He opened his eyes and held her gaze for a long moment.

"How could I not?" she whispered, leaning closer to caress his cheek. His soft stubble prickling the tip of her fingers. "I couldn't just let you die."

"Have you told Robin about me yet?" he asked, his voice strained.

"I figured you should tell him yourself," she said, holding his gaze. "When you come back home with me."

"Home with you?" He let his face fall into the palm of her hand. "I thought you wanted me to leave?"

"I did." Her eyes filled with tears. "But that was before I almost lost you."

Will caught the tear that slid down her cheek, then rubbed his rough thumb against her skin. "You'll never lose me."

She pressed her face into his warm palm and closed her eyes. The feel of his skin against her cheek was soothing, and she just wanted to melt into him. "I'm sorry about all of those terrible things I said to you."

"I deserved them," he said, his warm breath brushing her face. "And I'm sorry for all the pain I caused you. I wish I could take it all away. I wish I weren't a wolf."

"I don't care that you're a wolf, Will," she said, opening her eyes and meeting his gaze again. "I just hate that you lied to me. And that you didn't trust that I would accept you for who you are."

"But your hatred for wolves—"

"For *one* wolf," she clarified. "I've only ever hated the wolf that killed my grandmother, and I never knew they shifted into human form. This changes everything. The way people will perceive you—"

"No." Will's voice was as firm as he could manage while still in pain. "You can't tell people we're shifters. Otherwise, it'll be harder for us to hide."

"But that's what I'm saying." She offered him an encouraging smile. "You don't have to hide anymore."

Will mirrored her smile as he caressed her cheek. "As much as it relieves me to know that I don't ever have to hide from you again... it still doesn't change *this*." He lifted the blanket to expose his wound. "I got shot with an arrow even after I helped save the people, Red. Wolves aren't wanted. We'll never be."

She put her hand over his and lowered the blanket, covering the wound. "That was just

Robin being Robin. Besides, he didn't know it was you."

Will laced his fingers with hers. "There will always be a *Robin* out there. No matter what I do, and how much I prove myself, they will always look to kill me."

"Yeah, well…" She looked at their hands laced together. "They will have to get through me first."

Will smiled, his expression relaxed as if the pain had finally subsided. "I love you so much," he whispered, and she turned to meet his eyes. "I've been in love with you for as long as I can remember."

Her cheeks flushed, and his smile grew wider.

"You picked apples for your grandmother every morning by Crystal Lake," he said, pushing a strand of hair from her eyes. "And I would just watch from a distance, trying to muster the courage to talk to you."

"Why didn't you?"

"Because I had just started shifting, and my brother didn't think it was a good idea to let a human girl find out about me."

"Well, that's not fair." Red pouted. "Belle's

human, and according to Levi, she knows the identity of most of the pack."

Will smiled. "Yeah, but Belle rescued my brother from a wolf trap that almost cost him his life. Despite knowing he was a wolf, she still treated him and healed him back to health. After that, she sort of became the pack's physician. In fact, they bickered like siblings. So much so, whenever he came to her with an open gash from a fight, she would use the remedy that burned the most as punishment for fighting." Will chuckled at the memory. "That was always funny to me."

His warm expression fell, and he looked at their entwined hands again. It was the same look every time he talked about his brother, but now she understood why. He blamed himself for his brother's death.

"Levi told me about your brother," she whispered. "That he was the alpha, and that he saved your life."

Will's jaw tightened, and she wondered if maybe she shouldn't have brought it up.

"Sorry, we don't have to talk about it."

"No, it's okay," he said. "I don't want any more secrets between us." He caressed the back of her hand with his thumb, and she loved the way it felt. "There was a ball at Emmett's castle, he was just the Prince at the time. Belle was going, and my brother was worried about her. Something about someone being part of her fate or whatnot. They argued for hours. My brother wanted to escort her to the ball, but she didn't want him anywhere near that castle because Emmet was known for being a great wolf hunter."

"Why would she even want to be with a man like that?"

"Something about her story and The Intruder. I don't know. But even if that didn't work out, Marian is Emmett's sister, and her and Belle have been friends for years. Still, my brother followed her to the ball."

"What did *you* do?" Red asked.

Will lowered his eyes. "I followed them, and my brother caught me by the river. He told me to go back home, and as the alpha, I should've obeyed his command. But as my brother..."

"You didn't."

"How could I?" He shook his head. "My brother was walking into the castle of the most notorious wolf killer known in all the land. If anything happened, he would need help."

Red chewed her bottom lip nervously. "When did things go wrong?"

"When I looked in through the window of the kitchen," he said.

"You got caught stealing food?"

"Not just any food," Will clarified. "It was a tray with a variety of different apples. Some I had never seen before in the Chanted Forest. Others looked like they'd been dipped in gold, and all I could think of in that moment was..." He turned to meet her eyes. "How much *you* would like them."

Red's eyes widened. "Me?"

He nodded as the corner of his lips lifted a little. "I thought that if I brought those home, it would give me an excuse to talk to you. I would've given you every single one of them."

"Oh, Will." She leaned into him with a frown, hating the thought that it had all gone wrong because he was thinking of doing something nice for *her*.

"Anyway, when they caught me, I got scared and shifted. In the blink of an eye, hundreds of guards were surrounding me, and a minute later, Emmett came with his silver sword, ready to strike."

"What's a silver sword?"

"It's a sword made of elven metal that if any wolf is cut with, they don't easily heal from it. And if they do, it'll leave a nasty scar."

Red clasped his strong hand, wishing none of that were true. Wishing she could change his past and fixed all the heartache reflected in his eyes.

"My brother came out with Belle and Marian. He shifted in front of me. He was bigger and stronger than I was so... the smile on Emmett's face when he saw him was like he'd just found a treasure chest full of gold. Belle tried to talk Emmett down, tried to reason with him, but he wasn't budging. He wanted blood, and he wanted the alpha. My brother attacked enough of the guards to make room for me to run, but he didn't make it far." Will's eyes filled with tears. "I should never have left him behind. I should've stayed and fought with him."

Red cupped his face. "You were fifteen, Will."

"He died because I was a coward."

"You weren't a coward," she assured him, still holding his face in her small hands. "You just did what the alpha told you to do. Besides, it was Emmett who killed your brother, not you."

"Actually, it wasn't." Will lowered his eyes. "Last I heard, by the time the pack arrived, my brother was still alive, which means one of the wolves must've challenged my brother while he was injured in order to become the new alpha."

"Is that how it works?"

Will nodded. "Once a wolf defeats an alpha, they take their place."

"What about your banishment?" Red asked. "Why was that even necessary?"

"Because a wolf that's not part of the pack cannot challenge an alpha," Will explained. "And the new alpha probably knew I would eventually challenge him to avenge my brother's death."

"How do you beat an alpha, then?" Red asked.

"Either you wait for them to challenge you, or you kill them."

"I am so sorry you went through all of that."

Will kissed the back of Red's hand. "None of that matters anymore. As long as I have you by my side... nothing else matters." He cupped her face and pulled her close. "I love you, Red. I always have, and I always will."

His words somehow made the feeling even more real, and she suddenly felt the possibility of a lifetime together. In that moment, she knew she would do anything to make things work between them, even if that meant being rejected by her own people for loving a wolf.

She leaned into him and twined her arms around his neck as she rested her forehead against his. "I love you, too," she whispered. "And I don't ever want you to leave."

When his eyes darkened, she knew he recognized the intensity of her own love for him. She leaned down and pressed her lips to his neck. His skin was warm under the tip of her tongue. With a groan, he pulled her above him, and in a motion that felt utterly natural, she moved her mouth toward his. When their lips came together, the brush of his lips triggered a wave of pleasure, coupled with a riptide of desire more powerful than she'd ever experienced before. Without a second thought, she deepened the kiss, and his hands squeezed her waist. He then tenderly traced her stomach and trailed down her hips as if memorizing the feel of her body, even over her clothes, the sensation was as exquisite as anything she'd ever known.

Rushed footsteps barged into the room, followed by someone clearing their throat. Red ripped herself from Will.

"Sorry to interrupt," Levi said, his eyes glued to the floor. Red stepped away from the bed with her cheeks burning.

"How come you're back so soon?" she asked breathlessly. "Where's Belle?"

"It's been almost two days," Levi said, turning to Will. "And she wasn't home."

"What's wrong?" Will asked, wincing as he sat up.

Levi hesitated, chewing his lip. "The alpha…"

"What about him?" Will pressed, his expression serious.

"The alpha has your sister."

Will jumped to his feet, grimacing as he

held the blanket around his waist. "Tell me everything you know."

"Will, careful." Red hurried to his side, examining the wound. It looked a lot better, but it still wasn't fully healed. "Please lay back down."

"I'm fine." He raised a hand, keeping his eyes on Levi. "What does he want?"

"For you to accept the challenge."

"What challenge?" Red asked, looking at Will. When Will didn't respond, she turned to Levi. "What does that mean?"

"It's a fight. If Will wins, he can become the new alpha."

"And if he loses?" she asked, horrified. "I thought you said the alpha didn't want to kill him? This doesn't make any sense. He's already banished. Why is the alpha doing this?"

"An alpha only has to feel threatened and that's enough to instigate a challenge," Will said, balling his hands into fists. "And now he has my sister, so if it's a challenge he wants… then that's what he'll get."

"Well, you're not going alone," Red said, reaching for her cloak, not caring that it was stained with Will's blood. "My bow and arrows are with Pedigree outside."

Will came to stand in front of her and cupped her face in his strong hands. "I'm sorry, Red." His voice was barely above a whisper. "But I can't risk anything happening to you."

She gave him a puzzled look. "What are you saying?"

Will leaned down and pressed his warm lips to hers. "You can't come." When he pulled back, it took her several seconds to register what he'd said.

"Wait, what?" Red watched him head toward the door. "Will, you are not leaving me behind! Will!"

CHAPTER 12

As Will raced through the forest in wolf form, he wondered whether the adrenaline pulsing through his veins was masking his pain, or if the strong-smelling poultice Red used on him had already healed his wounds. The misty morning wind whipped through his fur. Levi led the way, his ears pricked up every few minutes, and Will knew what he was listening out for. Being in wolf form during daylight was risky. If wolf hunters were to cross their path, they would attack.

But the alpha had Belle. The one living person in this world who understood Will. Who knew him better than anyone. She was worth fighting for. Even dying for.

His heart panged at the thought of losing the challenge and never seeing Red again. Just as he thought they were able to overcome all the obstacles and finally be together, the alpha had to go and destroy even that small seed of happiness. Now, the only way to get that back was if Will became the new alpha. But he didn't want to be the alpha. The thought of leading the pack filled him with uncertainty. He had always been an outcast, always hiding who he truly was.

Yet, now he was forced to confront his torrid past at full speed. This time, he was going to face his fears head-on and fight for Belle. Losing the challenge was not an option. Not only did it mean death, it meant he would have failed his sister and would no longer be around to have a future with Red. He gnashed his teeth and growled at the thought.

The saltiness in the air told him they were close. He caught the strong scent of the pack. The forest floor slanted, and moments later, he broke out of the forest and into a violent rain, his paws padding the wet grains of sand with relief.

The pack has been assembled in the arena. The alpha is waiting for you.

Levi's thoughts sent Will's heart racing. No formalities, no time to rest. The alpha wanted to fight. Now.

As they reached the edge of the beach, the ocean rolled in and pushed back like it was breathing. The ocean reflected the cobalt skies as raindrops dashed onto the water, rippling the surface. The weather had been cold and turbulent, but the splash of rain on his fur was a blessed relief. Will did not enjoy it for long, though. He turned toward the rocks where a narrow pier stretched out to a coliseum in the distance. He crossed the bridge, then entered into the sandstone arena and gazed up at the walls towering over him.

He had heard stories about this place. The Gladianton arena was built in the ancient times. Every four years, champions from every kingdom from the seven seas would battle. The gladiator games had ended many years ago when the age of peace began, yet the arena still stood. It was abandoned like a relic, an ancient reminder of more perilous and brutal times.

It was the perfect location for a challenge. Will knew little about the true identity of the alpha. Since his banishment, he was forbidden to even get close. But whoever it was, it didn't matter. The alpha was going to lose the title and be forced to release his sister.

Will followed Levi through a large stone archway and found numerous stands in the shape of an amphitheater. Wolves of every autumnal shade sat with their black eyes watching his every move. A lone wolf with golden fur sat in the center of the arena and stared at him pointedly.

Levi took his place in the stands, and for a moment nothing happened. All was silent except for the rain slamming the sandstone and the swooshing of the tide. Will flexed his muscles and leapt to the center of the stadium. The alpha sat still, eyeing Will as if he were prey.

The wolves watched silently, no one daring to move. Even Levi's thoughts grew quiet. Will stopped and narrowed his eyes at the alpha.

Why did you call for me? he asked, but the alpha simply stared at him with a stern expression. *Why am I here?* When the alpha still didn't respond, Will roared. *Where is my sister?*

She's safe. The alpha's thoughts entered Will's mind in his own voice, much like Levi's thoughts had. Yet, the way they were said sparked recognition in his mind, but he couldn't quite discern from where. Or whom. *She will return to you as soon as you overpower me.*

Will's upper lip curled back as he snarled. *And if I don't?*

Then I'm afraid her fate will be worse than death. The alpha got up on two high legs, towering over Will. He jumped back and crouched in a defensive position. The two wolves circled the arena, heads low and shoulders hunched.

Why me? Will asked.

I made a promise to your brother.

Will snarled at hearing the mention of his brother from the mouth of his killer. *That was years ago... why challenge me now?*

I've been waiting... and now you're ready.

Will snarled.

Manners, Will. This is an alpha challenge. The golden wolf stopped and raised his head. *First, we bow.*

They both dipped heads. But before Will

could stand, the golden wolf swiped his paw, dropping him to the ground.

I can feel you trying to get in my head, the alpha snarled. *Quit it.*

Will stood and shook the sand off his fur. *Why are you keeping me out? What are you hiding in there?*

Why does it matter?

Will growled. *Because you killed my brother.*

The golden wolf swiped a paw, his claws snagging Will's fur like a comb. Will rolled over and jumped away with a painful yowl.

Howling echoed through the arena as the pack watched, exhilarated by the challenge. Will charged and shouldered the alpha, knocking him to the ground. He bared his fangs and launched, but the golden wolf swiped at his face. Will's cheek stung, but he shook the pain away and pounced again.

The alpha jumped to his feet, dodging Will's attack, then used his momentum to kick him to the ground. Sand scratched at Will's wound and he grimaced. The poultice had only done so much in the brief time he had to heal, but even injured, he was still strong enough to fight. He had to be.

Will pushed himself to his feet, watching as the alpha encircled him.

Do you want to know what happened the night your brother died? the alpha asked. *Fight me, and I'll tell you everything.*

Part of Will wondered if the alpha *wanted* to be defeated. But a larger part of his brain didn't care. He *needed* to win. For Belle. For Red. For his brother.

He lunged toward the alpha again, clawing at his shoulder. The golden wolf yelped as he dropped to the ground. Will dove toward his neck, teeth bared, but the golden wolf rolled out of the way, only to jump on Will's back and pin his face to the sand. The alpha grazed the edge of his razor-sharp claws over Will's jugular. One quick move and Will would bleed out. He pressed his eyes shut, waiting for the fatal cut to end his life. But instead, the alpha's voice entered his mind again.

Don't show your weakness, he said. But it wasn't a threat. Instead, it sounded like advice from a mentor.

The alpha pulled back, releasing its lethal

grip. Will dipped his head with a rumble as the golden wolf began circling him again.

When thrown down, you always get up with your head held high.

Will froze, shock shooting through his brain as those words echoed in his mind. He turned to meet the alpha's topaz eyes. Only one person had ever said those words to him.

Get up and finish the fight, the alpha commanded, but Will was too stunned to move.

He stared at the golden wolf in disbelief. *Belle?*

The alpha stopped and let out a long breath. *Now, why did you have to do that?*

Belle's voice entered Will's mind as her own, paralyzing him. He stared at the golden wolf in shock, noticing for the first time its feminine walk as it continued to circle him.

You're the alpha?

Don't get emotional. Her voice was stern. *Finish the fight.*

You... He stumbled back, blinking as if the alpha had thrown burning coals into his eyes. *You killed my brother.*

Your brother turned me into this, she hissed. *I*

never asked to become a wolf. Let alone an alpha. He gave me no choice. Now, fight!

Every ounce of energy drained from Will's aching body, and his mind began to spin. *The spices… the strong smell of the herbs… it masked your scent.* He looked up at her again, his mind reeling. *No wonder you were able to hide so well.*

She let out a frustrated growl. *Will, focus. I killed your brother. I banished you. Now, fight me!*

Will peered into his sister's glowing eyes. *He told you to kill him, didn't he?*

She shook her head. *Stay out of my head, Will.*

I see it clearly, now.

Belle jumped back, shaking her head as if trying to keep Will from entering her mind fully. *Stop it.*

The clouds parted and there was a break in the rain, and Will could only hear his own heart thumping against his ribcage.

He was injured and already dying. Her thoughts—her memories—were clear as the sky above them. *But he still bit you, injecting the venom into your bloodstream and transforming you into a wolf.*

Will, please. She crouched to the ground as

he invaded her mind, crumbling all of her defenses.

He summoned the pack then asked you to kill him in front of them. He staged a challenge just like this one because he needed you to become the alpha. He knew anyone else would've had me killed for disobeying his orders. He was protecting me. And so were you.

Belle looked up at Will with her eyes glistening in the sunlight as if full of tears. *Please…* Her voice came out soft and pleading. *Free me.*

Red's scent overtook Will's senses almost immediately, and he looked to his left. She was invisible, but he could sense her presence. Before he could refute his sister's request yet again, she charged toward Red at full speed.

Will bared his fangs and a deep guttural growl rumbled from the darkest part of his soul. He jumped on the alpha's back, clawing the wolf's hindquarters. He ached and agonized at knowing that was still his sister, but he also understood why it needed to be this way. The pack was watching. And respect needed to be earned.

Will scrambled onto the back of the alpha, throwing all of his weight down, forcing the wolf to fall. He pressed a paw onto its neck, feeling the rapid pulse beneath his skin as his sister panted under his weight.

Kill me, Will. Please. Free me from this guilt.

I won't kill you.

Belle let out a defeated sigh. *You must. It's the only way you can become the alpha.*

Not anymore.

Will pulled back and raised his eyes to the pack, who was still watching. *As of today, I am issuing a new rule. The alpha challenge does not have to be a fight to the death. Therefore, no one dies today.*

The wolves descended the stair-like stands and joined Will on the ground of the arena as a weak ray of sunshine poured in through the broken clouds and rested on Will. The pack formed a full circle around them then bowed before their new alpha.

Will looked down at his sister, who still hadn't moved, and nuzzled her neck. *You're free now.*

She whimpered as she nuzzled him back. *Thank you.*

CHAPTER 13

Red watched from across the arena as Will howled to the skies and the pack of wolves scattered, disappearing from sight. She jumped down from Pedigree and started toward the injured wolf, who was still lying on the ground, whimpering in pain. Will clearly won the fight, but why hadn't he killed the wolf yet? Maybe he was leaving it for her to finish him off, and that was exactly what she was going to do.

Red pulled her hood from her head, purposely making herself visible to the injured wolf. She wanted him to see her. To know who was going to kill him. And when their eyes locked, that was all Red needed to put an end to her revenge. She sucked in a breath, then nocked an arrow in her bow and pulled back.

But before she could release it, Will, who was still in wolf's form, stepped in front of the injured wolf and sat down, blocking Red's shot. She loosened her grip on the arrow and cocked her head at him. Was he protecting the wolf that killed her grandmother?

A surge of rage rose inside Red, and she gripped on her weapon again. "Get out of my way, Will. I am going to kill him, and you can't stop me."

Will's amber eyes frowned, and he whimpered a wordless plea not to do it. But it wasn't going to work. There was nothing he could say to her that would change her mind.

"No!" A voice came from behind Red, and she swung around. A woman with curly brown hair jumped down from Robin's horse and hurried to the golden wolf, who was still panting on the ground. Red stared at the woman and gasped with recognition. Marian. Red watched as Marian brushed the former alpha's fur.

Red dropped her hands and stared at

Marian's back. "Why on earth are you helping the creatures who kidnapped you?"

"She didn't kidnap me," Marian replied, examining the injuries of the wolf. "She took me from Prince John so I didn't have to endure a loveless marriage."

"*She?*" Red echoed, clutching at her weapon.

Robin came to stand next to his cousin. "We were on our way back to the village when we saw you coming this way. What on earth happened?"

Red wanted to respond, but her attention was fully absorbed by the wolf in front of her. Why was everyone helping that killer?

Will ran across the arena and returned with a cloak between his teeth, then dropped it at Marian's side. He then moved back with his brows furrowed as he watched Marian lean down and press her ear to the wolf's chest.

"She's got a few broken ribs, but I can't treat her here," Marian said to Will. "I need my healing kit."

"A healing kit?" Red hissed, looking from Marian to Will. "Why are you going along with this? That killer deserves to die!"

"Come on, Belle." Marian grabbed the cloak from the ground and covered the golden wolf. "You need to shift back."

"Wait…" Red's mouth dropped open. "That's *Belle*?"

The brown wolf stepped back and turned toward Red. Robin jumped in front of his cousin and put a protective arm in front of her.

"It's okay." She touched her cousin's arm. "He won't hurt me."

"And since when do we trust wolves?" Robin asked.

"He's not just any wolf," she said, pushing her cousin's arm down then glancing at the light brown animal. "It's Will."

Robin's eyes shot up, and neither of them said anything for a long time. He glanced over his shoulder at the brown wolf, and Will bowed his head.

Robin looked at Red, his face stunned. "Will is a *wolf*?"

Red wanted to respond, but she couldn't find her voice. She turned to look at Marian, who was still caressing the wolf's fur.

The golden wolf finally shifted into human

form, and Belle's dark brown braids came into view. Red's heart ached in her chest. Will lowered himself to the ground next to his sister, whimpering as if apologizing for having injured her.

"*Belle* is the alpha?" Robin echoed, his eyes even wider than before. Red wanted to correct him and explain that Will was the new alpha, but she still couldn't find her voice. *Belle* was the alpha. That whole time.

Red looked at Will, who was still whimpering next to his sister.

"It's okay, Will," Belle breathed, caressing Will's fur. "You did good. Your brother would be proud."

Will whimpered again, nuzzling her cheek.

Levi appeared from the woods with Belle's clothes, and Marian took them. "A little privacy, please?"

Will stood and backed away while everyone else turned their back on Belle. Will came to stand next to Red, and she mirrored his sad eyes. "Your sister..." Red breathed, still shocked. "She was the alpha?"

He pressed his face into her palm and shut his eyes. She caressed his fur instinctively, trying to ignore the anvil that weighted down her heart.

Red's eyes shifted to her friend, who by then was already fully dressed but still in excruciating pain. "Belle... killed my grandmother."

* * *

*R*ed made her way to the edge of Egret village. Her hair was still wet from the bath, but at least it wasn't cold anymore. The rain had stopped, and the cloudy sky had darkened.

She smiled at a family setting up a tent near a tree, and a wave of gratitude rose inside her at the hospitality Egret village had shown to them. It was kind of their neighbors to allow them to stay while Sherwood village was rebuilt. Again.

Red entered the house where Belle was recovering. The elderly woman who owned the hut wasn't home, but Red could hear Will's voice coming from the bedroom. She slowly made her way toward the sound, climbing the narrow staircase. She winced with every creak, not wanting to intrude. She listened to Belle and Will's voices trailing down the hall.

"I just wish you had trusted me with your secret," Will said, his voice downhearted. "I can't believe you've been carrying all this weight on your own."

Red reached the doorway to see Belle lying in bed with Will knelt by her side. A single candle burned on the nightstand, casting a soft glow across Belle's troubled face.

"It wasn't a matter of trust," Belle assured him. "And as for the banishment—"

"I know." Will reached for her hand. "You *had* to banish me as punishment for what I did."

"Not just that," Belle confessed, her voice weak. "I also didn't want you to hear my thoughts and find out that I was the one who took your brother's life."

Will shook his head. "It was a fatal wound from the silver sword. I know that now."

"True, but you were so young. I wasn't sure you would understand. I was also afraid you wouldn't let me look after you if you knew the truth, and I had promised your brother I

would. You didn't have anyone else but me."
She gave his hand a light squeeze. "I also
promised him that I would make you a leader
one day. When you were ready."

A silence followed, and Red wondered
whether to leave or enter the room. But then
Will spoke again, freezing her on the spot.

"What made you think I was ready now?"

Belle smiled. "Being with Robin has done
you well. He's a good leader because he knows
how to protect his people. Then I saw the way
you fought at Aria's castle. You went against
the pack to protect your friends, and I was
surprised at how many of them you over-
powered."

The answer hung in the air as Will stayed
silent. Even though he had his back to Red,
she could picture his furrowed brows and
thoughtful expression.

"Can I ask you a question?" he said,
finally.

Belle nodded. "Anything."

"What did you want the key for?" Will
asked. "The one we took from The Prince."

Belle cleared her throat then looked
toward the door. Will's eyes followed her gaze.

Red's face flushed. "Sorry." She let out a shy chuckle. "I didn't mean to eavesdrop, I just didn't want to interrupt."

Belle frowned. "Please, come in."

Red entered the room and pulled up a chair next to the bed across from Will. She stared at Belle for a long time. The answer to the one question that haunted her all her life was moments away, but for some reason, she couldn't bring herself to speak.

"I did kill your grandmother," Belle confessed, and Red let out a breath she didn't realize she'd been holding. "But I didn't mean to."

Red's eyes filled with tears.

"When I was first transformed into a wolf, I suffered from blackouts," Belle explained. "For a whole week, I was driven by nothing more than just instinct."

"What does that have to do with my Grams?"

A tear slid down Belle's cheek. "I went to her for help," Belle said. "She was a healer, and I wanted to know if there was any way to remove the wolf's venom from my blood before it was permanent, but…"

"You blacked out while you were with her," Red finished Belle's thought with a heavy heart.

"I am so sorry, Red." Belle cried. "There hasn't been a day that's gone by that I haven't thought of her. And what I've done."

Red lowered her head as a single tear slid down her cheek. "I believe you," Red said, her voice soft and filled with sadness. "I just wished you would've told me."

"I wanted to," she assured her. "These secrets were killing me. But I didn't know how."

Red lifted her eyes to meet Belle's. "I'm going to need time."

Belle nodded. "I understand." She then turned to Will with a serious look. "Which is why I need you to do something for me…" She sucked in a breath and looked Will in the eyes. "I need you to banish me from the pack."

"What?" Will jumped back, her words repelling him. "How can you ask me that? Absolutely not."

"Will, listen to me…" She pushed herself to sit up. "I never asked for any of this. Your brother took it upon himself to hand over his responsibility to me, and as much as I understand why he did it, that still wasn't fair to me. So, now that you're the alpha, I need to focus on getting my life back. That key you took from Prince John... that will get me a step closer to finding the antidote so I can get rid of this *beast* inside me, once and for all."

Will shook his head. "I'm sorry, Belle. I can't do it. I can't banish you."

"Will…" Belle reached out her hand.

Will stooped down and took it reluctantly.

She pulled him close. "No matter what happens, I will always be here for you. But I have my own path to follow, and you have yours."

"I don't know anything about being an alpha," he mumbled, lowering his head.

"But you do know loyalty," she said with a smile. "And that will make you a great leader."

Will let out a low grunt then touched his neck as if something had bitten him. He frantically looked to Red as he began gasping for breath.

"Will?" Red rushed to his side and caught

him as he stumbled forward. "What's wrong with him?"

Belle let out a similar grunt before dropping her head back on the pillow with her eyes closed.

"Belle?"

Will collapsed and Red eased him to the floor. "Will? What's happening?"

His eyes rolled back, and he passed out.

"Will!"

"He'll be fine." A man entered the room with heavy boots, and Red looked over her shoulder.

The Sheriff of Nottingham.

"What did you do to them?" Red hissed, still holding Will in her arms.

"It's just a sedative to tame the beast," he said, his voice calm as he looked at Belle. "So pretty. What a shame."

"What do you want?" Red said acidly. "Wasn't burning our village enough for you?"

"Oh, haven't you heard?" he asked, walking around the room, pretending to inspect for dust. "Robin Hood was charged with arson. There are eyewitness accounts that he started the fire that destroyed the village.

He and his conspirators will be hanged at dawn."

Red wailed, prompting a sickening smile from the sheriff.

"That's right," he said, finally turning to look at Red on the floor. "Coming for you and your *pet* was our last stop. Can't risk having any threats on the loose. Guards!"

Two guards hurried into the room. "Yes, sir."

"Take them away."

"Should we take the woman too, Sheriff?" one of the guards asked, motioning to an unconscious Belle.

"No, you can leave her." The sheriff waved it off. "Doesn't even look like she can stand."

One of the guards took Red by the arm, while the other threw Will over his shoulder.

"You're not getting away with this," Red hissed.

The sheriff flashed her a wicked grin. "We'll see about that."

CHAPTER 14

*W*ill woke up with a pounding headache. His limbs were heavy as he rolled onto his back and looked up at the damp ceiling. A steady drip echoed, magnified by the cold empty cell. A grumble caught his attention, and he spotted Robin sitting in the corner. Red sat by his side, rubbing his back, seemingly lost for words.

As he pushed himself to sit up, his body ached and a grunt escaped his lips. The sound prompted Red and Robin to turn in a flash.

"Oh good. Sleeping beauty has risen." Robin jumped to his feet. "Hurry up and break us out of here."

Red dashed to Will's side. "Are you okay?"

she asked, lifting his shirt and checking on his wound. Her face relaxed when she noticed it was fully healed. Still, her hands stayed on his skin and her touch reignited a fire within his chest. His heart swelled as he looked into her worried eyes.

"I'm fine," he said, grazing her cheek with his thumb as he cradled her face. Red moved to clutch his wrists, and the two of them held eye contact for a long time. Recent events had them both reeling, and neither of them needed to utter a word to know exactly what the other was thinking. Her eyes turned glassy as the corner of Will's mouth pulled upwards.

"What has gotten into you two?" Robin's words snapped them out of their moment, and Will dropped his hands. "Will, do your wolf thing and get us out of here."

"Where are we?" Will asked, getting to his feet.

"We were blindfolded, but I'm pretty sure it's one of Prince John's dungeons," Robin said.

Will strode to the bars of the cell, but then stepped back and eyed them warily. *Elven metal.*

A cut from this material, even a graze,

could be deadly to a wolf. The silver sword that killed his brother was made of the same metal. There was no way he would be able to get them out of that cell, not even as a wolf.

"What are you waiting for?" Robin asked impatiently.

Will's shoulders dropped with a sigh, and he shook his head. "I can't."

"You're not even going to try?" Robin asked, panic seeping through his tone. "Look, the Sheriff of Nottingham has framed us for burning down the village. And he's taken Marian, which means the wedding is back on."

Will's stomach knotted. "This may be hard for you to believe, but Marian is not the only thing in this world that matters."

Robin balled his fists, ready to pounce on Will, but Red shouldered her way in between them and pushed Robin back.

"Now is not the time to be fighting." She shot Will a sour look. "Or instigating a fight. Now, Marian is marrying The Prince in less than forty-eight hours. We still have a chance—"

"We'll be dead by then," Robin grumbled,

glaring at the stone floor. His words echoed like whispers around the dark corners of the cell, sending shivers down Will's spine. He studied Robin's face, and to his disappointment, he could tell this was not another one of his dark jokes.

"What are you talking about?" Will asked.

Robin dragged a hand across his face with a huff. "The Prince has ordered that the perpetrators of the fire be hanged at dawn."

Will and Red shared a look.

"And... that's *us*?" Will asked.

Red paced the cell, loosening her braid as she chewed her lip. "They can't just execute us without proof. Or without a trial."

Robin snorted. "You know how corrupt the system is. They can do whatever they want. Besides, we're wanted thieves."

Red collapsed on the damp floor and pulled her legs up, wrapping her arms around her knees as the news sunk in. Robin mumbled something unintelligible then turned toward the bars.

Will joined Red on the floor and pulled her into his arms. Her small frame molded against his chest as he held her tight. The pull to kiss away all of her sorrows grew stronger by the second. She looked up at him, and without another thought, he dipped his head and pressed his lips to her ear.

"We have to tell him," he whispered, and she pulled back, eyes wide.

"Now?"

Will shrugged. "Looks like we're going to die soon, anyway."

"What are you two whispering about?" Robin muttered.

Will stood and looked at Robin. "There something else you should know," he said, his voice calm.

Robin narrowed his eyes. "What?"

"Red and I… we're in love."

Silence washed over the room for several seconds, then Robin gasped, his tone dripping with sarcasm. "I am in utter shock."

Red jumped up and took Will's hand in hers. "It's true."

"Of course it's true." Robin gave his cousin a lopsided look. "The whole village has taken note of how you two look at each other. Seems like the both of you were the only ones too blind to see it."

"Really?" Red looked at Will, her cheeks flushing with color.

"Yes, now can we please focus on how to get out of here?" Robin turned toward the bars again. "Wait, did you hear that?"

The sound of hurried footsteps made the three of them pull away from the bars and fall silent. Will's ears pricked up and he sniffed, surprised he hadn't picked up on the person approaching from farther away. But Red's sweet scent flooded his senses, and it was difficult to focus on anything else with her in such close proximity.

The jingle of keys announced the arrival of someone, but there seemed to be no one there. Will peered through the dark bars to the empty corridor. Only the soft glow of a candle lit up the end of the hall as it rounded a corner.

"Who's there?" Robin asked, his voice firm. Will sniffed again and focused. Whatever was in that poison dart had drowned his senses. He shook his head with a frown, then a wisp of a new scent took his attention. There was something distinctly familiar about it.

Red gasped, throwing her hands over her

mouth as she looked ahead. Will followed her line of sight and flinched. Little John appeared in front of the cell, wearing Red's cloak. With the hood down he was no longer invisible, and he busied himself with picking the lock.

Robin watched him skeptically, but Little John paid no attention. He did not even lift his gaze as he wiggled two pieces of metal into the lock. When it clicked, he pulled the cell door open with a triumphant laugh.

Robin followed Red and Will out of the cell but stopped in front of Little John.

"I'm on your side, Robin," Little John assured him. "I've always been."

A proud smile spread across Robin's face, and he put a hand on his friend's shoulder. "Glad to have you back."

"How did you find us?" Red asked.

"Belle," Little John said. "She had some of the pack track you all here. She also gave me your cloak." He looked at Robin again. "When I heard about the hanging, I knew I had to do something."

Robin nodded then clapped Little John's shoulder with a nod. "You just saved our lives.

Thank you. Now, can we go before we get locked up again?"

"We can't just leave," Red said, putting her cloak on like a cape then resting her hands on her hips. "The palace is teeming with guards, and everyone is expecting a hanging in the morning. Now Marian is being forced to marry that horrid prince."

Robin turned to Red, his shoulders squared and a glint in his eye.

"I know that look," Red said, the corners of her mouth lifting. "What are you plotting?"

Robin grinned fully as his eyes flitted between them all. "Now that we have your invisible cloak, getting Marian out of that castle won't be as hard as we thought."

Will stared at him, impressed by his friend's ambition but doubtful he could pull it off.

Robin's eyes glinted again as he flashed his teeth. "Come on." He clapped. "We've got a wedding to crash."

CHAPTER 15

*R*ed threw her hood over her head and followed a royal carriage through the gates, leaving behind a crowd of villagers standing outside. Thankfully, the castle balcony was empty. The wedding hadn't yet begun.

Red snuck past the guards and into the castle. It didn't take her long to find Marian's room. Despite the cheerful maids around her, Marian's expression resembled that of someone going to a funeral instead of a wedding. She stood in front of a full-length mirror, staring at her long white gown. Red couldn't even fathom what Marian must've been feeling. Not only was she about to marry a man she didn't love, but her brother practically sold her in exchange for The King's allegiance.

But none of those things needed to happen. Not if their plan worked. All Red needed was to get Marian alone, then she would grab her by the hand, make her invisible and sneak out of the castle before anyone noticed she was gone. Perhaps, if she went into the washroom that would be the perfect opportunity.

The door swung open, and the women in the room fell silent. The Prince entered and waved a hand.

"But, Your Majesty. We're not finished—"

He scowled at one of the maids. "What did I just say?"

The maid lowered her eyes to the floor then gave a slight curtsey. "Yes, Your Highness."

Once the maids left the room, The Prince went to stand behind Marian, who hadn't moved away from the mirror. He touched her arms, and she flinched, her expression twisting as if she had eaten sour grapes.

"You are beautiful," he said, looking at her

reflection in the mirror. "Look at me when I'm talking to you."

Her eyes lifted begrudgingly to meet his, and he smiled.

"Much better." He slid his hands to her waist, and she pressed her eyes shut, fighting against the temptation to recoil.

"Why are you here?" she asked, grabbing on to her dress to avoid touching him. Red could only imagine how much Marian wanted his hands off of her.

"I just got word that the thieves I had in my dungeon have escaped," he said. "So, just in case they come by, I would like for you to politely let them know that it is your wish to go through with this wedding."

"And if I don't?"

He flashed her a wicked smile as he twisted a strand of her hair around his finger. "Then I can't make any promises about your brother."

"I couldn't care less about your allegiance with Emmett."

"I'm not talking about Emmett."

Marian's eyes widened and her angry

expression changed into one of fright. "You promised—"

"You haven't been keeping your end of the deal now, have you?"

She whipped around to face him with a scowl. "You touch one hair on his head, and I vow—"

"What, you'll get kidnapped again?" The Prince laughed. "I know your mutt friends arranged the whole thing to set you free from me. Now, my only question is, does Emmett know that his sister has dealings with wolves?"

"Why are you doing this?" she asked, her voice barely audible.

"Why do you think?" he replied, still twisting her hair around on his finger. "Power, sweetheart. Take a look outside my gates. All those people. They aren't here for me. They're here for you." He brushed a finger on her cheek, and her jaw tightened as if she was trying not to pull away. "They will follow *you*, and that will be good for *me*."

"I'm already marrying you. What else do you want from me?"

"Nothing." He lifted his arms in mock

surrender. "So long as you become my wife, I'll keep my end of the deal. Are we clear?"

"Crystal." Her tight jaw didn't soften. "You can go now."

He stepped back with a smug smile. "I'll see you soon, my beautiful bride."

Once The Prince left, Marian crouched to the floor and wrapped her arms around her torso as if trying to keep herself from crumbling. As she started to cry, Red's eyes welled up with tears.

"Marian." Red pulled her hood from her head then went to crouch next to her. Marian blinked in surprise.

"Red..." Marian's eyes drooped, and she started to cry all over again. "I can't leave."

"I know. I heard what he said." Red put a comforting hand on Marian's shoulder. "But he hasn't won yet."

Marian shook her head, tears still sliding down her cheeks. "If I do anything to betray him, he will kill my brother."

"You won't have to betray him," Red said, giving Marian a reassuring look. "You just have to do exactly what I say, and he will never suspect a thing."

Marian gave Red a quizzical look. "What do you need?"

Red's lips lifted a little. "For now... just a guard's uniform."

* * *

The palace grounds were bursting with lords and ladies, and all manner of distinguished guests. Even at short notice, the royal wedding had attracted attention from all over the land. Red shouldered her way through the crowd to take her position next to Robin and looked up at the palace, waiting for Marian to make her appearance.

King Richard and Prince John stood on the balcony, waving to the crowds with identical smiles.

Marian finally appeared on the balcony, her white gown shining in the brilliant sunlight. A wave of applause erupted around Red and Robin as they watched from the courtyard, disguised as guards.

Red looked around for Will. Although she knew she wouldn't be able to see him since he had her cloak, she noticed most of the guards around them were no longer at their post, which meant Will was successfully carrying out his part of the plan.

"Remind me again why I shouldn't just pierce that fool with an arrow?" Robin muttered, impatience evident in his tone.

"Because…" Red whispered, adjusting the baggy uniform over her petite frame. "He has leverage over Marian, and he won't hesitate to use it. Besides, if we keep taking her by force, this vicious cycle will never end. We have to be more subtle this time. And since subtlety is not your forte, please, leave it to me."

He grumbled, knowing Red was right. "Where's Will?"

"He knows what to do." Red gave her cousin a pointed look. "The question is, do *you*?"

Robin rolled his eyes. "Yes, ma'am."

"Good, because this just might be our last chance." Red sucked in a deep breath. "Here we go." She climbed to the top of a royal carriage just below the balcony and removed her helmet.

The Prince's eyes widened as he spotted

her looking up at him. "Guards!" he called out, his voice high pitched like a baby throwing a tantrum. "Seize her!"

Red looked around. There were no guards left on the ground floor. She wasn't entirely sure what Will had done to them, but it was perfect timing. She looked back up at The Prince and scrunched her nose. "Sorry, but I think you have a security problem."

The Prince scowled at the guards next to him on the balcony. "What are you waiting for, you fools? Get down there!"

The guards marched back into the castle, leaving only the sheriff on the balcony, standing behind the royal family.

"We come in peace," Red said, shifting her attention to King Richard, who was standing next to his brother. "All we ask is for an audience with Your Majesty."

"Now is hardly the place or the time for this," The Prince barked.

"Please, Your Majesty," Red pleaded, still addressing The King. She removed her bow and arrow then tossed them on the ground. "We come merely looking for justice."

"Guards!" The Prince yelled again, and a

handful of guards came rushing from within the castle with their swords drawn.

"Wait." The King raised a hand, bringing the guards to a halt.

Red bowed her head respectfully. "Thank you, Your Highness."

"Richard, don't listen—"

The King raised another hand, and his brother fell silent. He then shifted his attention back to Red. "I'm curious what matter could be so pressing. Proceed," The King said with a calm and controlled voice.

"We would like to inform you that your brother, The Prince, sent his men to burn down our village and framed Robin Hood," Red began. "And now, we have no roof over our heads, not enough medicine or food to eat. Your people are injured and starved."

The King hummed and leaned over the balcony edge. "Young lady, you are aware that the accusations you make are punishable by death if found false?"

Red nodded. "Yes, my king. I speak the truth... and I have proof."

The King turned to his brother, whose

face had drained of all its color. "What do you have to say about this?"

"It is nothing but a false accusation," The Prince responded, scowling down at Red. "They are merely a group of thieves looking to get out of their death sentence at the gallows."

"Don't take my word for it, Your Majesty," Red added, pointing to the crowd behind her. "Ask the people outside these gates."

The King's eyes shifted to the people. Even though he would most likely not notice the grayish color of their skin and hollow eyes because of the distance, their silence said it all.

"I am going to ask you one more time," The King said, turning to his brother. "Are these allegations true?"

The Prince's cowardly eyes shifted to the sheriff who stood behind them. "It was you, wasn't it? You burned down their village."

The sheriff's eyes widened as he looked from The King to The Prince, beads of sweat sliding down the side of his face as he gulped loudly. "Yes, sir. I did."

"How dare you?" The Prince yelled, pretending not to have known anything about it. The sheriff lowered his eyes to the ground, accepting the blame.

"Robin Hood and his merry men had taken The Prince's bride, my lord," the sheriff said, his voice shaking. "I was just acting in the name of justice—"

"Enough." The King raised a hand, and The Prince swung around with eyes wide as he looked at his brother. "How could we expect our people to rejoice in today's union when we have caused them so much pain?"

"My thoughts exactly," Red chimed in. "Which brings me to the next reason we've come today."

The King turned to Red with narrow eyes. "And what reason might that be?"

"Retribution must be made," she said. "And as subjects to your kingdom, we believe Your Highness will provide your people with the proper restitution as well."

The King was silent for a long moment, and the crowd muttered to each other. "What are your demands?" The King said, finally.

"We want materials to rebuild our village and food for our people."

Red tried to ignore the stares all aimed at

her and kept her focus on The King, who hummed as he scratched his jaw. His brows knitted together to form a single fury line across his forehead, and for a tense moment, Red wondered if she had gone too far. But she kept her shoulders squared and stood tall, willing The King to agree.

Finally, The King nodded. "I am a compassionate king. Of course, I will help the people of Sherwood. I will have my finest men rebuild the village and will send food and supplies to all who have been removed from their homes."

Sighs and cries of delight crossed the crowd like a wave. "Long live King Richard!" they chanted.

Robin then climbed up to stand by Red and shouted up to the balcony. "And we request that you free Princess Marian."

"Robin, not yet," Red hissed. "We haven't even bargained for our lives yet."

Robin didn't respond, he just kept his eyes on The King. Hushed whispers flew around the people as everyone stared at Robin with disapproval.

Robin ignored them. "I propose a challenge," he said to The King. "For the freedom of Princess Marian."

The King looked at Marian, and she lowered her head.

"Very well," The King replied. "If you win, Princess Marian may have her freedom."

"But Richard—"

The King raised a hand to stop his cowardly brother from saying anything further, then met Robin's eyes. "But if you lose, you and your friends will be taken to the gallows and executed tonight."

Robin sucked in a breath. "Deal."

"Robin!" Red turned to her cousin with a horrified expression. "We agreed on banishment, not death, you overconfident fool," she hissed.

"Relax," he muttered under his breath. "And have some faith in your own plan, will you?" He then shifted his attention to The Prince. "You may pick any target which I must retrieve using *one* arrow. That is the challenge."

The King gave a nod of approval then looked at his brother. "What will it be?"

Marian leaned in and whispered into The

Prince's ear. Red didn't have to hear in order to know what she was saying. The Prince flashed a smug smile as he turned to look at Robin.

"The target will be..." The Prince's smile grew wider. "The coin inside my back pocket. You retrieve *that* using one single arrow, and you win."

"Are you sure that's the best you can do?" Robin teased, his voice calm, and as always, overconfident.

Red stomped on his foot with frustration.

Robin winced then gave his cousin a pained look. "Okay, fine, that was a bit much," he grunted before stretching out his hand. "Hand me my bow and arrow, please?"

Red handed his bow and a single arrow.

Robin squared his shoulders then nocked his arrow in his bow, closing one eye to perfect his aim. Red pressed his quiver to her chest and stopped breathing.

Robin shot the arrow. It grazed The Prince's arm then crashed through a window and disappeared into the castle. For a moment, everyone looked stunned, including

The Prince. But then a wide smile grew on his face.

"Well, look at that," he said with a smug smile. "You missed."

Robin lowered his bow then flashed a smile in return. "Did I, though?"

The Prince's eyes widened as his body stiffened. He looked at his hands but he couldn't move them. His eyes found Robin again moments before he dropped to his knees then collapsed to the ground.

"There is nothing to fear, Your Majesty," Robin assured The King. "The paralysis will wear off in less than a day."

"Paralysis?" The King echoed.

"Yes, My Lord," Red chimed in. "It's from the adronna plant."

Robin flashed his cousin a smug grin. "That was brilliant. Now, if you'll excuse me. I have a coin to retrieve." Robin jumped down from the carriage then climbed the lattice. Red followed him until they both reached the balcony. After rolling the paralyzed Prince on his belly, Robin bent down and retrieved the coin from his back pocket.

"Your Majesty." Robin turned toward The

King, coin in hand. "The target as promised. The deal was to *retrieve* the target using one single arrow. He never said it needed to be hit *by* the arrow."

The King took the coin with a sour expression, certainly embarrassed to have been outsmarted.

Marian screamed and Robin whipped around to find the sheriff with a sword over her neck.

"You think you're so clever, don't you?" the sheriff hissed.

"Put the sword down," Robin demanded. "And fight me like a man."

"You are done making fools out of us," the sheriff said, pressing the sword a little deeper. "And since you don't want to pay for your sins, then she will have to pay them for you."

"Will…" Red called out, sitting up on the ledge. "Can you please do something about this?" Suddenly her red cloak appeared behind the sheriff, resting on the back of a massive brown wolf. Will snarled, inches behind the sheriff's head.

Red then looked at the sheriff and smiled.

"I would listen to him if I were you. He can be very persuasive."

The sheriff slowly lowered his sword and Marian ran into Robin's arms. At that, the sheriff took off running into the castle.

"Are you okay?" Robin asked, looking for any injuries.

"I'm fine," Marian said, pulling back and smoothing her dress. She stepped over The Prince, who was still lying paralyzed on the ground, and joined Red by the ledge.

Robin turned toward The King and bowed his head. "Thank you, Your Majesty. And my apologies for the fear-inducing methods. It will not happen again."

"You are a brave young man," The King said, moving toward Robin. "Reckless and foolish. But brave, nonetheless. And rest assured that even though I will keep my word today, if you are *ever* found within my property again, it will be the end of your life. Am I being clear?"

Robin stiffened a little. "Yes, Your Majesty."

"Good." The King pulled back then looked down to the guests. "My beloved friends, there will be no wedding today. This royal event is now over, and I wish all of you to go home."

The gates rolled open, and the shocked crowd dispersed as The King gave one last glance at Princess Marian. "Best wishes to you." He then disappeared into the castle.

Robin let out a long breath as Red rushed toward Will, who was still in wolf form. He licked her face, and she didn't protest this time.

"So…" Marian walked toward Robin. "You won my freedom."

Robin smiled. "You're welcome."

"As a sign of gratitude, I supposed I should give you something, say… well-deserved?"

Robin's smile grew wider. "That would be lovely." He leaned in to kiss her, only to get a slap in the face.

"What was that for?" He touched his reddened cheek.

"For kidnapping me in the first place, then bringing me back here," she said bitterly. "And for being so reckless with everyone's lives."

"To save *you!*"

"Reckless, nonetheless." She huffed then

marched across the balcony. "Will, can you take me to Belle, please? I need to check on her injuries."

Will lowered himself to the ground, and Marian climbed on his back as if mounting a horse. As he rose, his amber eyes met Red's.

"I'll see you back at home," she said, caressing his snout. He licked her hand before jumping off the balcony and landing gracefully on the grass. As he ran towards the woods, the pack that had been hiding in the forest followed after him.

"So…" Red leaned on the ledge next to Robin. "How does it feel to finally get the girl?"

Robin watched as Marian disappeared into the woods. "I *will* win her heart, Red. You'll see."

"And that clarity came before or after the slap in the face?" Red teased. "Just curious as to your degree of delusion here."

He bumped his hip on hers, and she laughed.

"All kidding aside…" Robin said. "I'm proud of you."

"Me?"

"Yes, you." He turned to face his cousin, still leaning on the ledge. "Your plan was brilliant. And it couldn't have worked out any better. You're the one who saved everyone today."

"I'm just glad everyone is okay."

"Also..." He flashed her a proud smile. "You're not a little girl anymore. And I couldn't think of a better man for you than Will. Even if he's a mutt."

Red smiled, giving her cousin's arm a tight squeeze. "Thank you. It means the world to me to hear you say that."

"Well, I guess it's time then."

She gave him a quizzical look. "Time for what?"

"For the talk."

"The talk?" Red spluttered, raising her brows at him.

Robin nodded. "*The* talk."

Red's face turned crimson. "Oh, no we're not." She whistled, and both her horse and Robin's came galloping from outside the palace gates.

"Red, you're not a little girl anymore, remember?"

"I am not listening." She jumped onto the lattice and clambered down as quickly as she could.

Robin followed after her, suppressing a laugh. "Red."

"Still not listening." She mounted her horse with flushed cheeks and Robin laughed as he mounted his steed next to her.

"It's too easy to make you squirm," he teased.

"I'll race you to the village," she challenged with a smug grin.

Robin beamed. "You're on."

CHAPTER 16

The sun set behind the crest of a hill as Will bounded forward, heading for the village. A soft golden glow flooded the sky and Will couldn't help the grin from taking over his face. If anyone had seen him, a grinning wolf, they would have run away, or laughed. Will wasn't sure.

His heart soared at the knowledge they had won. The sheriff confessed to his crimes. No more gallows at dawn. No more chasing after Marian. No more secrets. It was time to rebuild and look to the future. A future with Red.

The neighboring village was half a day's walk from Sherwood. Every tavern, inn, and dwelling was packed with people. Egret village was known for its hospitality, despite having very few resources. The people had pitched tents for the unlucky villagers who could not find a place to stay. Will had been able to secure a small room above a blacksmith's shop.

Will heard a victory laugh come from Little John as soon as he entered the tavern. A group of men sat in the center of the tavern, clanging their drinks and spilling the clear liquid on the wooden table. Though Robin was sitting among them, he didn't seem to be sharing in the merry celebration.

Will squeezed into the group and took a seat next to Robin. He downed his drink, probably not his first, then looked across the room. Will followed his gaze and spotted Marian shooting darts in the corner with Red.

"This is a disaster," Robin mumbled. "She hates me."

"Why do you say that?"

"Because she was living in Pearl Island under a different name, and when I came looking for her, I revealed her true identity to the people," Robin explained. "They wanted nothing to do with anyone related to King Emmett. Or Prince John, for that matter. So, they made her leave."

"Ah, I was wondering how you'd gotten her to come with you."

"More like she was forced to leave because I blew her cover." Robin downed yet another drink. "Now, she won't even look at me."

"She won't look at you because you keep treating her like she belongs to you."

"But the book said—"

"*That you belong together,* I know." Will put a hand on his friend's shoulder. "But she hasn't read the book, and the only Robin she's met so far has been the rough-on-the-edges version that we all love to hate. So, you give her some time to catch up. Maybe even show her your softer side."

Robin gave Will a hard look. He didn't seem to care for the advice, but he knew Will was right.

"So, what do I do?" Robin asked. "Go over there and teach her to play darts or something?"

Will shrugged. "Why don't you start by asking her if she would like to be taught?"

"Why would I ask that? The woman clearly has no idea what she's doing." Robin pointed in her direction. "Either that or she's been told by some moron that the dart needs to go on the wall."

"I'll tell you what…" Will slapped Robin's shoulder. "I'll go over there and say something nice about you. You know, soften her up a little before you come over."

Robin nodded. "That's actually not a bad idea. You can tell her I'm a terrific kisser."

Will narrowed his eyes. "I think that would be a little too obvious considering I wouldn't know. But hey, don't worry…" He slapped Robin in the back a second time then stood. "I'll put in a good word for you."

As Will made his way toward Red, his smile grew wider. "Hey, beautiful." He dipped his head and gave her a kiss on the cheek.

Red smiled. "Good timing. Can you please help me convince Marian to stay?"

Marian rolled her eyes playfully then went to retrieve the darts she had pierced on the wall just above the board. "I'm sorry, Red, but I can't."

"You keep saying that, but you haven't given me a reason."

When she turned around, her eyes flickered toward Robin as he downed yet another drink. "I don't care what someone has written about my life. I want to choose my own destiny."

"We're not asking you to stay for him," Will added, wrapping his arms around Red as he stood behind her. "We're asking you to stay because we need your help."

Marian cocked her head. "What do you mean?"

"You're a healer."

"And?"

"Many of our people are suffering with burns from the fire," Red explained. "They're in desperate need of remedies that we just don't have any knowledge of. You would be a tremendous help to them."

Marian paused to think about it before nodding in agreement. "Fine, I'll stay."

Red squealed as she jumped up and down.

"But…" Marian raised a finger then gave Will and Red a serious look. "As soon as they're healed, I am out of here."

"We'll take what we can get," Will said, lowering his voice. "And so will *he*."

Marian stole another brief glance at Robin, then averted her eyes to the darts in her hand. "I don't think your cousin is a bad person, Red." Marian lifted her eyes to look at Red. "I do admire his fearlessness and bravery very much."

"Then why do you keep pushing him away?" Red asked.

"Because I grew up around many iron-fisted men," she explained, turning toward the dartboard. "So, now that I am finally free for the first time in my life, I have no desire to be anchored down with someone like that." She threw the dart with a bit too much force, but again it missed the board and pierced the wall.

"I can understand that," Will said. "But Robin isn't iron-fisted. He's just hard-headed. But even that is only on the outside. Inside, he's the epitome of mush."

"Let me guess…" Belle approached, taking a dart from Marian's hand. "You're talking about Robin?" She threw the dart and hit the bullseye on the board.

"Please don't tell me you're also infatuated

with this whole book thing?" Marian gave her friend an exasperated look.

"The only reason you're not is because you haven't read the book," Belle said, glancing at Robin across the room. "If you had, you would realize that our friend over there is as fragile as a dandelion flower."

"He would kill you for saying that, you know," Will added.

The girls laughed, and Robin gave Will a puzzled look from across the room. Will shook his head, silently telling him not to worry about it.

Belle turned to Will and touched his arm. "Can we talk... alone?" she muttered, looking at him intently. Will followed her out of the back door, and the two of them stood in the dim alley.

"Is everything okay?" he asked as she turned to face him.

"I really need you to banish me from the pack," Belle said, catching Will off guard. And her serious expression told him she wasn't joking.

"Why?" he asked.

"Because it's time, Will." She bit her lip and looked away.

Will's frown deepened. He thought Belle could tell him anything. Especially now that there were no more secrets between them.

Or was she hiding more?

"What about the pack?" Will asked, rubbing the back of his neck.

Belle looked at him again, her eyes teary. "They follow *you* now, and they need you to lead them. But I can't stay. There's something I have to do. Alone. And please, don't ask me why. I can't tell you."

Will opened his mouth to argue, but Belle gripped his arm and gave him a pleading look. "Please, you just have to trust me. I wouldn't ask you to do this if it wasn't important." She stared him down until he finally sighed.

"Fine." He gave a curt nod. *Belle, you are hereby banished from the pack.*

A distant howl answered the call, and Will's stomach clenched at the thought of his sister leaving for good. Belle leaned forward and pressed her head against Will's forehead. He closed his eyes, and the two of them stood there silently for a long moment. Then, when they broke apart, tears clung to her cheeks.

"Take care of them, Will," she whispered.

"I will, I promise."

* * *

*W*ill returned to the tavern, wondering if he might finally get a chance to be alone with Red. As if to answer a prayer, he spotted her walking out, and his heart leapt.

"Hey, where did you go?" she asked.

He grabbed her by the hand. "Come, I have something I want to show you." Will guided Red across the village square then stopped just short of a small wooden door. He stepped behind her and covered her eyes.

"Will?"

"No peeking," he whispered into her ear, pushing the door open with his foot. The floorboards creaked under his weight as he made his way to a small room lit by nothing except a lantern in the corner.

"Okay, ready?" He uncovered her eyes, and she gasped.

"Will…" She spun around the cozy bedroom with a wide grin. "Is this for me?"

"Well, considering the amount of work it took for me to put it together, I say it's just as much mine as it is yours," he teased.

She put a cute hand on her hip and narrowed her eyes at him. "Will Scarlet, are you saying you want to share your living quarters with me?"

"I'm saying…" He pulled her close and circled her waist with his hands. His touch sent a rush of color to her cheeks. "I would like to build a life with you." He peered into her eyes, and a shy smile spread across her lips.

"And how do we go about doing that?" she asked, suppressing a grin.

"Well, first… I would have to claim you." When she arched a brow, he gave it a light shrug. "It's a wolf thing."

"I see." She threw her arms around his neck and held his gaze. "And how exactly does *that* work?"

"Very simple," he said, gently brushing her dark hair out of the way then tugging at her shirt until her left shoulder was completely bare. "I would just mark you right... here." He leaned down and pressed his warm lips to her bare skin, then he pulled back to look at her again. "And just like that, every wolf on the planet would know that I belong to you."

Red sucked in a breath as if breathing became suddenly difficult. She had untied her braid, and a spray of loose hair fanned across her narrow shoulders, and the top two buttons of her cotton shirt were undone. The thin material barely concealed her form, and as Will's eyes looked down, his mouth went dry. Red pushed his chin with a finger, forcing his mouth to close and his eyes to meet hers.

"You make traditional rings sound so boring," she teased with a wry smile.

"What can I say, it's just not permanent enough," he said, tightening his arms around her. "Besides, it's only fair considering you've already marked me."

She gave him a quizzical look. "Are you sure you're not confusing me with Robin?" she joked.

"I'm not talking about the arrow to my ribs," he said, reaching for her hand. "I'm talking about what you've done to my *heart*."

He placed her palm against his muscled chest, and her breath got caught in her throat. "You've claimed it forever. Now, it only beats for you."

Red's smile faded at the intensity of Will's stare. The embers of desire that had been burning quietly in the background were suddenly set ablaze. Will couldn't decide if it was the wolf side or the human side that magnified his passions, but he didn't care. He longed to taste Red's lips and caress her bare skin. The thought heated his whole body, and the urge became all-consuming. He needed her, and the heat in her eyes told him she needed him just as much.

As if reading his thoughts, Red tentatively traced a line from his forehead, down his right temple and over his neck. Her hand again hovered over his heart.

"Your pulse is insanely fast," she whispered.

Will swallowed hard as he let his gaze settle on Red's bottom lip. It beckoned him to nibble it.

Instead, he searched her eyes, making sure she was just as hungry as he was. He took a fistful of her hair and pulled her in, hovering just an inch from her lips to give her one last chance to push him away.

Red closed the gap and claimed his mouth. He lifted her off the ground, and she wrapped her legs around his waist. The weight of her body pressing on his hips sent Will's senses wild. He moaned against her lips and ran his hands under her shirt, caressing the soft skin on her back. Red's hands held Will's face as they shared the most passionate kiss Will had ever known. Red opened her mouth to invite him in, and Will obliged, deepening their kiss. The sweet, familiar scent of Red took over his senses and made Will want to howl.

He squeezed her thighs, checking that she was real and not some figment of his imagination. He pressed her up to a wall and she threw her head back with a sexy grunt, wrapping her arms around his neck. Will grinned.

"I love you, Will," Red whispered, breathless.

She claimed his lips again, her nose nuzzling his cheek. Will took his free hand and dragged it through her hair. Every cell of his body shuddered, and his muscles tensed. He couldn't work out if kissing Red was making him feel more or less frustrated. He turned, bringing Red with him, then threw her onto the bed. She fell back with a dark smile and arched her body as she watched him prowl toward her.

Will zoned in on Red's delicious scent, wanting so desperately to feast on it. He inhaled deeply, enveloping himself in her, and propped himself up on his elbows, hovering over her trembling body and nipping her bottom lip again.

Then, a cough broke the moment, and Will wrenched himself from Red's lips.

Little John hovered by the open doorway, his face ashen white. "I'm sorry for inter-rupting…"

"Is it urgent?" Will asked with a slight grunt.

"It's Robin," he said, his voice wavering.

"Just tell him we'll meet up with him later," Red said. But Little John shook his head faintly.

"Robin's been taken."

Red's expression turned serious, and she

squirmed from beneath Will to sit up on the bed. "What do you mean *taken?*" she asked, and Will stood.

"Look—" Little John shakily held up a piece of parchment. Will took it from his hand to look at the words.

A howl of thieves brings the captor to his knees. A touch of frost and all is lost. Only true love's kiss will return that which you miss.

Will looked up to frown at Little John as Red took the parchment. "I don't get it."

"I found this outside the tavern." Little John held up Robin's quiver and arrows.

Will exchanged looks with Red as she stood. Will stormed past Little John and ran out into the street. Red and Little John followed.

"Will, wait!" she called after him.

Will stopped at the edge of the forest and scanned the pairs of eyes glowing in the darkness. He turned back as Red fastened her cloak. "You can't just go running after him. We need a plan."

"I can track him. I'll take the pack and—"

"Did you not read the note?" Red asked.

Will huffed and dragged a hand over his face in frustration. "What do you mean?"

"*Only true love's kiss will return that which you miss,*" she paused. "What are you planning to do? Hunt him down and kiss him?" Red placed her hand on his shoulder, and immediately a rush of calmness washed over him.

"The message is cryptic," Little John said, holding up the parchment again. "Maybe your sister would know."

"Belle's gone," Will said.

Red looked at him in surprise. "Gone where?"

"She wouldn't tell me. But we're going to have to figure this one out on our own," he said with a sigh. "What do you think we should do?"

"Me?" Red glanced at Will then at Little John. "Why are you both looking at me?"

"Well, Robin was usually the one who came up with the plan. Now that he's gone... this should be given to you," Little John said, handing over Robin's bow and quiver. Red took it and stared at it for a long moment. Then she looked up at Will and squared her shoulders.

"We need a team." She looked toward the forest.

They were surrounded by Will's pack, and he wondered if she knew they were listening.

"Little John, start recruiting more men. We're going to find out who took Robin and what they want with him. We need to get him back."

"My pack will join you on your quest," Will said, taking Red's hand.

"We should have a name," Little John muttered, scratching his bearded chin. "How about The Wolf Bandits?"

"No. We're not going to do any more stealing," Red said firmly. She pulled out an arrow from Robin's quiver and inspected it.

"From now on," she said, setting the tip of the arrow on fire. "We'll be called... The Red Arrows."

She threw the arrow on the ground and stepped on the flame.

Will smiled then turned to his pack. With only his thoughts, he gave them instructions to track Robin's scent and find out what they could about his capture. Meanwhile, Red told

Little John to go back into the village and begin recruiting immediately.

Finally, the two of them stood alone in the woods and turned to face each other. Will took both her hands and drew closer. "Don't worry," he whispered, studying her troubled face. "We're going to find him."

"I know, I was just thinking that…" She paused and looked up at Will. "Robin got so obsessed with the story The Intruder gave him," she said. "But his story is different now. So, I can't help but wonder… is there a story about us too?"

Will brushed her bottom lip with his thumb and smiled. "Red Ryding Hood and the Wolf," he said tenderly. "Sounds like an epic story to me."

Red reached up and placed her hands around his neck. "Red Ryding Hood has fallen in love with the wolf—who saw *that* coming?" She smiled back at him.

Will lifted her in the air and swung her around. After setting her down and brushing a strand of hair away from her face, he kissed her softly. "For the record," he whispered against her lips. "The wolf loves her back."

EPILOGUE

$\mathcal{B}$elle entered Prince John's wedding ball disguised in a beautiful light blue dress. It had been a long time since she had worn a corset. The boning kept her back perfectly straight and she could hardly breathe. Nevertheless, she picked up her heavy skirts and plastered on her best smile as she walked among the dancing lords and ladies.

As much as she would like to have given her condolences to the young new bride he found to take Marian's place, Belle held back the urge by focusing on the real reason she was there.

The Prince began to dance with his new bride in the center of the room. She had a painfully narrow waist and a mass of blonde curls sitting on the crown of her head. She looked at Prince John with sparkling eyes, dazzled by her new husband and perhaps marveling at her luck. The guests' attention was respectfully glued to the couple as they formed a circle around them. Belle headed to the double doors that led to the garden. But before she could grasp the brass handle, a hand grabbed hers and turned her around.

"Fancy meeting you here," King Emmett said with what he must've thought was a charming smile. He had a finely groomed head of light brown hair and a square jaw, but his smile did not reach his eyes. His charms didn't work with her in the past, and they weren't about to work on her now. "Where are you off to in such a hurry?"

"I'm not in a hurry," Belle retorted. Her voice was slightly higher than usual, but Emmett seemed not to notice.

"Good." His smile grew wider. "Then you wouldn't mind doing me the honor of a dance?"

"Actually, I *do* mind." She pulled away

from him. "Now, if you'll excuse me, I need some fresh air."

She turned toward the double doors again, but they flung open and in walked the sheriff. She spun around before the sheriff could recognize her. After all, he'd seen her with Will and Red the night they were captured.

"On second thought." She grabbed Emmett's broad hand and dragged him to the very center of the dance floor, which by that point had filled with couples dancing around The Prince and his bride. She picked a spot out of the sheriff's line of sight and allowed Emmett to lead.

"So, what are you really doing here, Belle?" Emmett asked as they swayed together. "Because it can't possibly be for Prince John. We all know he's too much of a cad for your taste."

"No wonder you're such good friends."

He narrowed his eyes. "And yet, you're dancing with me."

She gave an innocent shrug. "I figured I already had the invitation from your sister's wedding, so why not?"

At the mention of Marian, Emmett's expression grew serious. "Have you seen her?"

Belle nodded. "She's doing well. No thanks to you, of course."

Emmett looked away from Belle, and she wondered what it was he didn't want her to see in his eyes.

"Spare me the guilty conscience act," Belle said, capturing his attention again. "I see right through you."

"Is that right?" He flashed her another smile then twirled her around before pulling her into his arms again. His light blue eyes peered into hers. "And what do you see?"

"I see..." she whispered, holding back tears as memories of that night flooded her mind. "A killer."

He let out a dry chuckle. "Hate me all you want, but I did you a favor by killing that beast."

Belle bit back against tears at his words. Will's brother was *not* a beast. "He was the most loving—"

"Until you got on his bad side," Emmett spoke through gritted teeth. "Don't you get it? No matter how nice or kind they may seem while in their human form, those beasts are wild savages. And if you get in their way, they will maul you without hesitation."

Belle was taken aback by the degree of hatred in his tone. Though she'd heard him say those exact words years ago, moments before he pulled out his silver sword and ran outside to the garden, she had never noticed the pain behind them until tonight.

"What did the wolves do to you, Emmett?"

Emmett stopped dancing and stepped back with another charming smile. Though this time she could tell it was a mere mask to hide the truth.

"Thank you for the lovely dance. Always a pleasure." He took her hand and kissed it lightly before walking away.

As she watched him leave the main hall, she couldn't ignore the nagging feeling that he was hiding something. Not that it surprised her. Emmett had never been known for his honesty. And it wasn't like she didn't have her own secrets. After all, she hadn't come for the wedding at all.

She looked around for the sheriff. He had

settled by the banquet table, talking to a young lady who looked far too young and innocent for a man like him. But Belle couldn't be bothered with such insignificant matters at the moment. She gave one last glance around the ball then headed to the double doors.

The starry night was cool and clear, and an unnatural calmness filled the air. It was a stark contrast to Belle's thumping heartbeat, drumming against her ribcage.

She held her breath as she struggled not to trip on the hemline of her dress or stumble over the gravel. Her body tensed with every step, and as she left the walled gardens, her ears began to ring.

After hurrying into the darkened woods behind the palace, she followed the trail until she came to a willow tree. Kicking the autumn leaves aside, she found an iron door handle on the ground. It was heavy as she yanked on it, and the door dropped open with a thud. She gave one last look around to check that she was alone then climbed down the iron ladder to a dark underground tunnel.

She took one of the flaming torches from the wall and pressed on. The flames danced on the rocky walls around her as she walked, and her anticipation grew to a fever pitch. After rounding two corners, she finally came to a thick iron door. Without wasting any more time, she pulled out the key she'd taken from Snow at Aria's castle and stared at it for a long moment.

It was made of elven silver with ancient markings branded on the side. She envisioned this moment for so long, and now that it had arrived, she took a moment to regain her composure. She sucked in a ragged breath, both excited and nervous.

"*Finally*," she exhaled, resolved and ready to face whatever she might find. She gritted her teeth as she forced the key into the lock. *There was no going back now,* she thought as she turned the lock. She listened for the sound she knew would come. And then it clicked.

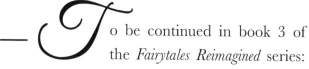 —*T*o be continued in book 3 of the *Fairytales Reimagined* series: *Beastly Secrets.*—

Read Now

Want to share fan theories and join the Fairytales Reimagined community? Come and join us on Facebook for funny memes, games, giveaways and be the first to see cover reveals. @fairytalesreimagined